Wade Masters said calmly. "I *give* it."

"Congratulations," Jana said with commendable aplomb. "Not many people could say the same." Or would want to, she added silently.

This man was going to be hell on wheels. "Lean and mean, smooth and sexy." That was her secretary's latest description of the ultimate male, and it fit Wade Masters right down to his neatly trimmed fingernails.

Lean? Definitely. Sitting behind a desk hadn't softened the sharp angles of his face or the lines of his well-knit body.

Mean? If that meant tough, direct and aggressive, yes, indeed!

Smooth? Yes, she'd give him smooth. His brown hair, sun streaked and stylishly cut, fell in natural waves, and the creases in his cheeks would probably be devastating when he smiled.

Sexy? Lord, yes. From the well-shaped mouth and firm chin, past the tailored navy three-piece suit to the gleaming leather shoes, he was every inch an elegant pirate. He was a disturbing man and, when he turned his attention to a particular woman, probably lethal.

It was a good thing their relationship was strictly business!

Dear Reader,

Although our culture is always changing, the desire to love and be loved is a constant in every woman's heart. Silhouette Romances reflect that desire, sweeping you away with books that will make you laugh and cry, poignant stories that will move you time and time again.

This year we're featuring Romances with a playful twist. Remember those fun-loving heroines who always manage to get themselves into tricky predicaments? You'll enjoy reading about their escapades in Silhouette Romances by Brittany Young, Debbie Macomber, Annette Broadrick and Rita Rainville.

We're also publishing Romances by many of your all-time favorites such as Ginna Gray, Dixie Browning, Laurie Paige and Joan Hohl. Your overwhelming reaction to these authors has served as a touchstone for us, and we're pleased to bring you more books with Silhouette's distinctive medley of charm, wit and—above all—*romance*. I hope you enjoy this book, and the many stories to come.

Sincerely,

Rosalind Noonan
Senior Editor
SILHOUETTE BOOKS

RITA
RAINVILLE
The Perfect
Touch

Silhouette *Romance*

Published by Silhouette Books New York

America's Publisher of Contemporary Romance

To Marge and Jim Eslick, my parents
—They would have been proud.

SILHOUETTE BOOKS
300 E. 42nd St., New York, N.Y. 10017

ISBN: 0-373-08418-8

First Silhouette Books printing March 1986

America's Publisher of Contemporary Romance

Printed in the U.S.A.

Books by Rita Rainville

Silhouette Romance

Challenge the Devil #313
McCade's Woman #346
Lady Moonlight #370
Written on the Wind #400
The Perfect Touch #418

RITA RAINVILLE

grew up reading truckloads of romances and replotting the endings of sad movies. She has always wanted to write the kind of romances she likes to read. She finds people endlessly interesting and this is reflected in her writing. She is happily married and lives in California with her family.

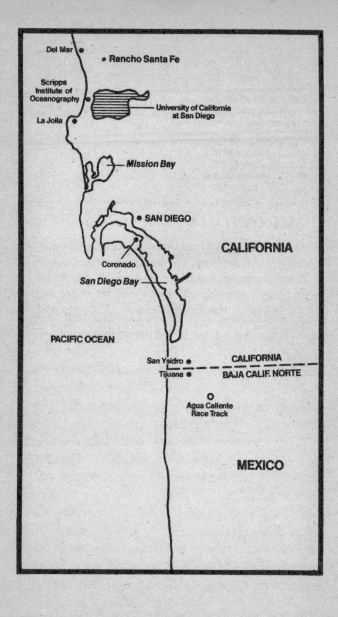

Chapter One

I don't *have* stress," Wade Masters calmly told Jana Cantrell, his deep voice ruffling her nerve endings. "I *give* it."

Jana blinked, and stared at the rays of San Diego sunshine shafting through the miniblinds of the man's large, cluttered office. Sheer determination and willpower kept her jaw from falling.

"Congratulations," she said with commendable aplomb, her hesitation barely noticeable. "Not many people could say the same." Or would want to, she added silently.

Why me? she wondered piously, absorbing the matter-of-fact expression in the man's dark eyes. I water old Mrs. Krispin's azaleas when she totters off to the wilds of Africa, I feed stray cats, and I run to the aid of my eccentric relatives, so why, of all of the people at the clinic, do I have to be the one he asks for?

The large, tawny-haired man eyed her thoughtfully. "In the electronics field, stress comes with the territory. You either learn to cope or you're eaten up."

"It's obvious that you're a survivor," she observed dryly. "But what about those who work with you? And for you?"

"That's why you're here. I talked to Bert Elkins the other day and he recommended you."

Jana's smile was rueful. "And did he tell you that he fought me every step of the way?" His blank expression was answer enough. "Obviously he didn't. Did he at least tell you how I work?" She leaned back in the chair with a soft sigh. Obviously he hadn't.

"Did he fight clean?" he asked, a flicker of amused interest in his brown eyes.

Her working relationship with the old and crochety Mr. Elkins had best been described as unarmed warfare. A cold finger of premonition skittered down her back as she eyed the man sitting behind the wide, dark desk. Mr. Elkins, worthy opponent that he was, had been a piece of cake. This man, alternately described by those who should know as a shark or a barracuda, would be hell on wheels!

Lean and mean, smooth and sexy. That was her secretary's latest description of the ultimate male. And it fit Wade Masters right down to his neatly trimmed fingernails. Lean? Definitely. Sitting behind a desk hadn't softened the sharp angles of his face or the lines of his well-knit body. Mean? If that meant tough, direct and aggressive, yes indeed! Smooth? Yes, she'd give him smooth. His brown hair, sun-streaked and stylishly cut, fell in natural waves that a good many women would kill for. The creases in his lean cheeks would probably be devastating when he smiled. Sexy? Lord, yes. Cathy would love him. In fact, Jana decided, it was a good thing he had used the telephone. If he had walked into the clinic, her young and highly susceptible secretary would have been rendered speechless and more than likely useless. From his well-shaped mouth and firm chin past his tailored navy three-piece suit to his gleaming leather shoes, he was every inch an elegant pirate. He was, she granted, a disturbing man; and when he directed his attention to a particular woman, probably lethal. Cathy was welcome to every devastating inch of him!

"Well? Did he?" he prompted.

She blinked, then remembered that they were discussing Mr. Elkins. "He fought to win," she told him.

"What was it, arm wrestling over morning coffee or a chase around his desk to get his blood stirring?"

"Don't laugh," Jana warned with a smile. Now that it was over, she had fond memories of their daily confrontations. "That scrawny old man will probably outlive us all. Our battles, by the way, were all in the line of business." Before he could distract her, she slid in another query. "Aside from his recommendation, why did you call me?"

Wade pointed to a stack of ledgers and thick reports. "That's why."

Tilting her head, Jana looked at the untidy pile. It wasn't any more informative from this angle than it had been before, she decided. "How many guesses do I get?" she asked.

Tapping the top folder with a silver pen, he said, "These are studies telling me what I already know. My sales campaigns have been successful. My business has nearly doubled. The current facilities are inadequate and the new ones are almost completed."

"And?" she prompted with a nod of understanding.

"And that's where you come in. Any one of those factors is enough to cause stress."

"Combined, they're lethal," she added succinctly.

"My employees need help, and in the San Diego area your clinic has a good reputation for providing it. I want you to work with my people."

"And you?" Jana ventured. "You're never bothered?"

His eyes held hers as he shook his head. "Never. I told you before, I'm the cause of it. Not intentionally; it's just the nature of things. I design the product, then my salesmen go out in the field and try to break the stranglehold the Japanese have in the electronics field. They bring in orders, and my production crew tries to meet the deadlines. Then the shipping people get in over their heads."

"The domino effect," she murmured.

He nodded. "Exactly. One department after another is caught up in the mess. It has to stop."

"And I have to stop it." It was a statement rather than a question. They both knew that was why she was sitting in his office.

"You're the expert," he agreed.

"Which brings me back to my earlier question. Did Mr. Elkins tell you how I approach a situation like this?"

"No."

She leaned back and eyed him speculatively. "I go beyond the conventional methods of stress management. The usual trio of biofeedback, instructional seminars and behavior modification is only a starting point."

He nodded and glanced at his watch.

Jana continued, ignoring his less than subtle hint. "I never take on a corporation unless the owner agrees to let me examine the work environment of the plant." She hurried on as he stiffened. "I look for stressors such as noise and crowding in work areas, inadequate lighting and ventilation, psychological burnout, and poor communication between workers and management."

"Wait just a minute." His voice was soft.

Here it comes, she thought with resignation. The velvet glove and the fist of flint.

"I'm hiring you to reduce stress," he told her. "Not to restructure the entire company."

"You're *trying* to hire me," she reminded him. "You want me because I get results. This is the way I get them. I'm telling you now because I don't want you to have any unpleasant surprises down the road."

"Did you have this discussion with Bert Elkins?"

Jana nodded an affirmative.

"Then why the daily arguments?"

"Because he agreed to my conditions, then fought like a wounded buffalo every time I moved into a new area. I don't want to go through that again."

"And if I don't agree?"

"Simple," she said with a steady smile. "I don't come." Not by the flicker of an eyelash did she betray the nervous flutter in her stomach. It was one thing to act unconcerned, she told herself, entirely another to be foolhardy.

Stubborn, Wade decided, eyeing her smile with interest. It was confident. She was good, and she knew it. She wouldn't even blink one of those ridiculously long eyelashes if he didn't hire her. What she probably *would* do was remove her fetching bottom from the chair and walk out of the office without a backward glance. And that, his body was informing him with increasing urgency, was the last thing he wanted her to do.

She wasn't beautiful. But she was the most astonishing combination of sensuality and freshness he had ever encountered. From the widow's peak in her cloud of auburn hair down to the high-heeled concoction of straps and soles that passed for shoes, she was one sexy lady. He wondered if she knew exactly how sexy she was. Not once since she had entered his office had she played on her femininity. Her slightly slanted hazel eyes were wide and direct. Her smile was much the same. No, he realized, while she was working she would rely on her skills, not her gender. He wondered suddenly if she would bring the same direct approach to a man's bed. To his bed.

Her voice raised his contemplative gaze from the soft rise and fall of the silky blouse beneath her suit jacket. "Well," she asked, "do you want me?"

A glint of amusement lightened his eyes. Yes. Direct and to the point. "On your conditions?" he queried gently.

She crossed one knee over the other and looked back with a slight smile, composure in every movement. "Of course," she agreed.

"Tell me more about them."

"I'm not demanding that you sign over your company," she sighed. "I'm not even asking for a carte blanche. I'm simply saying that if you want to do more than slap a Band-Aid on the problem, certain areas have to be examined."

Pointing out the obvious, she reminded him, "You're the owner, Mr. Masters. You wield the power. As a consultant, and with your approval, I examine, analyze and advise. As I go through the plant, I adjust to the rhythm of each work area, observing without interrupting. After all, my job is to reduce or eliminate stress, not increase it." Her shoulders lifted in a small shrug. "That's about it." The silence that followed seemed to indicate that the next step was up to him.

"I have a couple of conditions of my own," he told her.

Her dark brows rose in inquiry.

"First, I want you to call me Wade."

"I didn't call Mr. Elkins Bert," she objected.

"He's got almost fifty years on me," he reminded her. "And if I know him, he probably didn't ask you to."

"You're right. But it gets too complicated in a company like this, trying to remember when to call someone by their first name and when to use their last." Besides, she added silently, I have a feeling that I can use every bit of distance at my disposal.

He nodded agreeably. "I believe in keeping things simple. That's why everyone here calls me by my first name. Wade." His look was a silent challenge.

"Wade," she capitulated, disguising her reluctance. "What's your second condition?"

"That you have lunch with me."

She tested the statement cautiously. "Every day?"

"Today."

Jana glanced at her watch. "I have an appointment—"

"So do I, but I still have to eat, and so do you."

"You're right again," she admitted, as she rose in one smooth movement. "And there's nothing I like more than sticking my employer for the lunch tab." She tilted her head consideringly. "Or have I jumped the gun? Are you hiring me?"

"I am," Wade assured her. He poked a button on his intercom and said, "Sue, I'm going to lunch now. I'll be back by—" he checked his watch "—one-thirty." He looked at Jana. "We can go in my car. When's your appointment?"

"At two."

He nodded and held the door open. Jana walked past him, smiling grimly as the image of a lamb, followed by a large, lazily padding lion, etched itself in her mind.

"So what do you do with yourself when you're not straightening out the kinks in people?" Wade asked over the discreet ring of cutlery and crystal.

"You mean what do I do for entertainment?"

He nodded.

Jana unearthed a fresh mushroom from her chef's salad and looked up. She had lost count of the questions he had asked during the short drive to the restaurant, not one of which had pertained to business. She dipped the mushroom in a blob of creamy dressing and chewed it thoughtfully. Earlier, under the "mean" category, she had mentally listed tough, direct and aggressive. Now she added fast. He was moving at an alarming rate—straight as an arrow toward her.

This man was a perfect example of the type of complication she could do without, she reminded herself. With her usual precision she had neatly, if loosely, outlined her goals for the next several years. The clinic was her immediate concern. Almost a year ago she and her three partners had plucked their various framed degrees from the walls of a multi-storied medical building, rented a suite of offices and let it be known that their specialty was reducing stress in the corporate world. Now the clinic's reputation was growing, and so was business. Success was rewarding, but she had long since realized that it was also demanding. A couple more years, she'd decided. She would dedicate that much time to work, then do something about her personal life. So her plans, long-range or short, did not include a certain local business tycoon who was wickedly attractive and altogether too sure of himself.

Her decision to keep him at a distance was obviously going to have to be reviewed. Not that she had changed her mind, she assured herself. It was simply that a game plan affecting another person ran into difficulty if the other person had no knowledge of it.

And it got rather dicey if that person, with or without knowledge of the plan, was not inclined to cooperate. Wade Masters did not strike her as a man who worked in concert with others unless their plans coincided with his. But he *did* strike her as a man who pinpointed a goal, aimed straight for it and, come hell or high water, attained it. The thought was less than comforting, because he seemed to be eyeing her as if she were a top priority on his list of current objectives.

"Well?" he prompted.

His unswerving attention was distracting, she decided, and not at all businesslike. "I spend a lot of time with my family and friends, and I enjoy several sports," she said briefly. "We should really set up an appointment for next wee—"

His brows arched. "That's it? Family? Sports?"

Her sigh was a soft sound of resignation. "I like Neil Simon plays. About that—"

"What else?"

"Dinner," she said through her teeth. "As in going out to. Now—"

His voice was soft as he interrupted. "With whom?"

"Men." The *of course* wasn't uttered, but it was there for the world to hear.

"Men, plural, or a man?"

"Usually one man at a time," she told him after a taut silence.

He leaned back with a grin. "What else do you like to do?"

"Throw darts," Jana said with a barely concealed glare, toying with the idea of announcing that she moonlighted as a mud wrestler in some raunchy joint.

She shot a quick look at him from beneath long brown lashes and changed her mind. He'd probably escort her to wherever they did that sort of thing and demand a free show.

"I also like walking along tree-lined roads, driving in the mountains, danc—"

"How much of that do you do with men?"

Jana stabbed at an olive. "Plural or singular?" she asked, not bothering to hide her rising temper.

"Any which way."

"A lot," she admitted. "I like being with men."

"Good."

"And just what does that mean?" she asked in sudden suspicion.

"Simply that I like being with a woman who likes men."

The expression on his tanned face was trying hard to appear innocent, she decided. It was a useless exercise; he probably hadn't been innocent since he was five. And somehow her statement had not come out the way she intended. It was true that she enjoyed sharing things with men, but men who were good-natured, pleasant and undemanding. She definitely didn't mean the kind who had an untamed quality lurking in dangerous dark eyes. In fact, if this lunch was Wade's idea of companionship, he invested the word with a host of new, unsettling meanings.

She put down her fork and looked directly at him. "I thought this was a business lunch, not a modern version of the inquisition."

"I just said lunch," he pointed out mildly.

She took a deep breath, then let it out slowly. She inhaled again, quelling a flare of exasperation. She was rarely driven to the point where she had to practice some of her own relaxation techniques. This man, she realized with no surprise at all, could prove to be hazardous to her health.

"I think we should be discussing things like when I'll start working for you," she said.

"When can you come to work for me?" he asked obediently.

"Wait a minute," she murmured, taken by surprise. She reached for her purse, then flipped through a well-used calendar, frowning as she turned one page after another. "It'll be a couple of weeks before I can come on a full-time basis, but if we can work it out, I'd like to see you sometime next week to discuss a few things."

"Fine. Is your family here in San Diego?"

"What?" A frown settled between her gently arched brows at the sudden change of subject. "That's it?" she asked. "Just like that? Business is over?"

"I asked, you answered," he said reasonably. "What's left?"

"I never had to prompt Mr. Elkins," she said in a dry voice.

"That's probably because our approach is different." Blandly ignoring her doubtful glance, he continued. "For instance, I like to know all about the people I'm working with. All in the name of business, of course."

"Of course," she echoed.

"Your family," he prompted. "Are they in the area?"

"My parents live in Malibu."

"No one closer?"

"An aunt," Jana said, glancing suddenly at her watch.

"Where does she live?"

"Rancho Santa Fe." Reaching for her purse, she said, "We'd better get a move on if we don't want to be late."

Wade motioned for the waitress to bring the bill. "That's where I live. Maybe I know her."

"No," she said abruptly. "You don't."

He took care of the bill with a credit card and followed her out to his sleek, gray car, eyeing her stiff back with interest. "How do you know? We might be neighbors."

"Possibly. But if you are, you still haven't met her. She's just in the process of moving. In fact, I'm helping her settle in tomorrow."

"Is there an uncle?" he asked as he opened the car door.

Jana stopped as if she had run into a glass wall. Now *there's* a question, she thought. Aunt Tillie and Uncle Walter had been a devoted couple. Uncle Walter had died eleven years ago. Unfortunately neither he nor Aunt Tillie had accepted the fact. He communicated with her almost daily. If life was especially interesting for either of them, they might chat several times a day.

She eased into the car, not looking at the man beside her, who was obviously waiting for an answer. Wade closed the door and loped around to his side. Maybe he'll forget he asked, she thought hopefully. Hope died a resounding death when he turned to her with a look of inquiry.

"It wasn't a difficult question," he prompted. "A simple yes or no will take care of it."

Life is not simple, she decided with an inward sigh. "Yes."

Twenty minutes later she was turning her car out of his parking lot, pointing it toward the clinic and thinking about her aunt. Tillie was a wisp of a woman with the energy of a dynamo. She was lovable, absentminded, eccentric in her dress, impossible to follow in a conversation when she was disturbed...and psychic. It was the psychic part that got to most people, Jana decided. It was certainly the part that got to her.

Until just a year ago, her silver-haired cousin, Kara Brady, had been the principal recipient of Aunt Tillie's spooky predictions. Jana had been an amused bystander. But exactly twelve months ago—to be precise, three hundred sixty-one days ago—Jana had received a telephone call from Kara. She had, she informed Jana, met a man. *The* man. Dane Logan. They were getting married. Jana had never understood if it was in spite of, or because of, Aunt Tillie. But most certainly she'd had something to do with it.

"Jana," Kara had told her, "the time has come for you to share Aunt Tillie."

"Kara," she had said in stunned horror, "I can't. I'd be a nervous wreck. She terrifies me with that stuff. And Uncle Walter would probably want to be my financial adviser. I can't handle that, even if you did make a bundle on that transistor whatchamacallit he told you about. I don't want to know when my water pipes are going to burst, and I'd probably never get into my car again if she so much as told me to be careful. I like to be *surprised*," she finished desperately.

"It's not that bad," Kara soothed. "At least, not once you get used to it. And it's not as if I'm deserting her. I wouldn't do that for the world. But I'll be doing—"

"Kara."

"—some traveling with Dane—"

"Kara."

"—and she needs someone—"

"Kara."

"—to look in on her. Besides, you've never really had a chance to know them. I mean her," she said quickly.

"Them. That's what you said: *them*," Jana muttered gloomily. "It's not just her. I think Aunt Tillie's great—from a distance. It's the package deal that bothers me. I swear to God, Kara, Uncle Walter talks more now that he did eleven years ago."

"What you have to do," Kara told her confidently, "is take it straight and strong."

Jana considered that statement with all the suspicion that it deserved. "Exactly what does that mean?"

"It's really simple."

Jana had pressed the receiver to her ear and rubbed away the crease that was forming between her brows. To the average person, "simple" meant easy, ordinary and uncomplicated. Experience had taught her that Kara didn't know the meaning of those words.

"Simple as in turning my whole life upside down?"

"What you do is spend the day with Aunt Tillie and—"

"A *whole* day?" She'd rather be staked out on an anthill. In Death Valley. Without water. In the dead of summer.

"That's the best way," Kara decided. "All you need is a little exposure. Are you free next Saturday?"

"Yes, but I'm not—"

"Good. I'll come by and pick you up around noon. It'll be better if you don't have your car. That way you can't—"

"No."

"—just drive away if you get nervous. I'll—"

"No. I won't do it."

"—come back about six to pick you up."

"You're going to leave me there *alone*?" Horror waged war with anxiety, and the battle was declared a draw.

"You'll love her," Kara had informed her blithely and hung up.

Now Jana pulled into the parking lot behind the cream stucco clinic building. She removed the ignition key and regarded it thoughtfully. Her madcap cousin had been right. Her aunt's bright blue eyes had gleamed with love and intuitive understanding. Her gentle flow of words had washed over Jana like a cool, sustaining fountain, and Uncle Walter had remained discreetly silent. It had taken her less than two hours to fall completely under her aunt's spell. That day Tillie had acquired a second niece who was staunchly supportive and fiercely protective.

Jana smiled ruefully. There was no denying, however, that it had affected her social life. She made it a practice to introduce her men—at least those she dated more than three times—to Tillie. The strong were skeptical; the weak fell by the wayside. The last one had ignored Tillie's warning to be cautious around a small red car. The very next day he had stood in the street, sweeping leaves out of the gutter. He had waved to his neighbor, who was driving her children home from a soccer game. She sneezed, lost control of her little red car, and he ended up in the hospital in traction.

Jana got out of the car and locked the door. She wondered how Wade Masters would get along with Tillie. Her eyes glinted with amusement at the thought. "He's just a man you work with," she reminded herself sternly as she walked toward the building. "And there's no reason for them to meet. Thank God!"

Later she would think about that and know for certain that precognition did not run in the family.

Chapter Two

"You're late," Kenneth Trale announced. His green eyes gleamed in satisfaction.

Jana darted a glance at the large wall clock. "Come on, Ken. It's only thirty seconds."

"Late is late," he reminded her, and brandished an open cookie jar beneath her nose.

Grumbling, she extracted a dollar bill from her purse and dropped it into the jar. "Who suggested this crazy rule anyway?"

"I did," Laura Mead admitted calmly, "after you'd been late for three consecutive weeks."

Tish Roberts asked no one in particular, "But has it accomplished anything besides subsidizing our Christmas party? After almost a year, she's still late for these meetings."

Ken broke the thoughtful silence. "But she's down to thirty seconds. If you remember, it used to be twenty minutes. I'd say there's been a vast improvement."

Jana dropped into the last of the four comfortable chairs encircling a large coffee table and looked at her partners with affection. They'd done it, she thought once again. Each Friday, at their weekly keep-in-touch meeting, she marveled at how the four of them had linked their divergent strengths and weaknesses and had forged a prospering business from little more than savvy and zeal. Now, according to their accountant, they had a diminishing debt and could afford to grant themselves larger salaries. That was gratifying, of course, but the true satisfaction came from the realization of a dream.

Jana glanced at the woman on her right. Laura had an inner calm that never seemed to falter; it had carried the group through more than one crisis. Her low, deliberate voice and gray eyes reflected serenity, but aside from that, Jana decided, she was pure dynamo. Her curly hair was a snapping red; her large-boned frame moved with deceptive speed. Mother of three, she was happily married and wanted her partners to enjoy a similar state of bliss. Lately she had been watching Ken and Tish with great interest.

Ken was a practicing idealist. He would rake his fingers through his long brown hair when he proposed a particular course of action. If any of them suggested that his idea was impractical, that it sounded nice but life just wasn't that way, his jaw would set. "Then we'll just have to *make* it that way," he would say.

Tish was the voice of reason, and her voice was usually saying, "But, *Ken*, it just won't work." Then

her blue eyes would widen as he explained how it could
and would. Once convinced, she usually implemented
the practical means of turning his dreams into reality.

Jana's glance had circled the table and now rested
on her own folded hands. She, in her own opinion,
was neither fish nor fowl. She had no outstanding
characteristic to offer the others. Her greatest contribution had been suggesting the partnership and prov-
ing that it was feasible. She worked hard, but so did
they. Her appreciation of the ridiculous often lightened the atmosphere, but none of them lacked humor. She lifted her head at the sound of Tish's voice.

"You know, the thing I like most about these meetings is the silent appreciation that Jana offers. I feel
brilliant and noble before she even says a word."

Jana grinned. "Don't let it go to your head. I always need a few seconds to convince myself that we're
actually here and solvent." Turning to Laura, she
asked, "What's on the agenda today?"

"Not much from me. Another week or so and I'll
be finished at IML. Everyone's anxious to cooperate.
What about you, Ken?"

"No problems. I'll probably be at Apex for a couple of weeks. Tish?"

"Everyone at Hart's seems satisfied. Just a few
things to clean up, then I'll be through."

Three pairs of eyes shifted to Jana.

"Why do I get all the troublemakers?" she wondered aloud. "First Mr. Elkins and now—"

"Wade Masters?" Ken's voice was bland. "You're
complaining about good old even-tempered Wade—"

"Masters," Jana completed. "Do you know him?
You *do* know him," she stated with certainty, her gaze

a composite of suspicion and exasperation. "So why did I end up with him?"

Ken raised a forefinger. "Number one, he asked for you." The rest of his digits joined the first. "Numbers two, three, four and five, *because* I know him, I wouldn't have taken him on for twice our usual fee."

"Is he that bad?" Jana asked gloomily.

"Not really," he said finally, taking pity on her. "But remember how when we started the clinic, we agreed not to work with friends? Well, he's an old college buddy. We go way back," he assured her. "Back to beer guzzling and nights of debauchery."

"What?" Tish looked up with interest.

"Go on," Jana prodded.

"What kind of debauchery?" Tish asked.

"Go on with what?" Ken inquired.

Jana sighed. "Details, idiot, details."

"Yeah," Tish agreed. "Tell us about these wild, riotous, licentious nights."

"I want to hear about the man," Jana said.

Tish nodded. "I'll settle for that. Describe the debauchee. Or is it debaucher? And don't forget the orgies. The most I ever got invited to was a toga party, and it was pretty dull stuff."

"For heaven's sake, will you let Ken get a few words in?"

Tish leaned back, her blue eyes gleaming with amusement. "I'm all ears. Just don't forget the orgies," she reminded Ken. "And kinky things."

Ken's voice was testy. "There were no kinky things."

"Not even one little—"

"No!"

"Will you, for God's sake, please tell me about Wade Masters?" Jana pleaded.

Laura's calm voice intervened. "Come on, Ken. Put Jana out of her misery. In fact, tell us all about our new high-tech, high-tension client."

Ken ran a hand through his brown hair, leaving tufts sticking out like a randomly constructed bird's nest. His eyes narrowed as he thought. "He's in electronics, of course. He always fiddled around with the stuff. A couple of years ago he invented—or modified—something to do with electric eyes. Apparently it revolutionized the field. He owns his own company, and it's a damned good thing because he's not cut out to work on boards or committees."

"A loner?" Laura asked.

Ken shook his head. "No. Far from it. It's more like a case of...temporary tunnel vision. When something catches his interest, it gets his total attention. He sees the end result and has no patience with objections or protests along the way. All in all, he's probably the most single-minded person I've ever known."

"Terrific," Jana muttered weakly. "You realize, of course, that he doesn't expect me to help *him*. He isn't bothered by stress. I'm there to save everyone else." She repeated some of her conversation with Wade.

"That sounds like him," Ken said with a grin. "He gets rid of his tension by driving everyone else crazy. He hasn't changed a bit."

"You can't imagine how that comforts me," Jana said dryly. "Thanks, friend, you've really made my day."

"Speaking of days," Tish interrupted, "isn't tomorrow moving day for Aunt Tillie?"

Jana nodded absently. A few weeks after she joined Tillie's fan club, she had taken Laura, Tish and Ken to meet her. That had been before the partnership had officially been formed, before they had even mentioned it to anyone. Tillie's greeting had electrified them all and made instant converts of the three visitors. Jana smiled, remembering how Ken had briskly thumped the gleaming brass doorknocker. The ring had dropped off in his hand, and he had been offering it to Jana as Tillie opened the door.

She had been dressed conservatively, for her, swathed in yards of multicolored fabric that might once have been a parachute. The material was held together with heavy gold braid, and aquamarine running shoes peeked out from beneath her draped floor-length skirt. Bright blue eyes assessed Jana's friends.

"Yes, Walter was right." The words were a relieved sigh. "He said the building on Torrey Pines Road would suit you." She frowned at their blank expressions. "Office space," she prompted, patting her silvery curls in a vain attempt to subdue them. "For your clinic."

She swung the door open wider. "Come in," she said, whisking the ring from Ken's hand and dropping it in a wicker basket. She tilted her head, waited for Jana to place an affectionate kiss on her cheek, then took off at a trot. "Sit in the living room," she called over her shoulder. "I'll bring the peppermint tea."

Three pairs of eyes turned to Jana. She held up her hand as if taking an oath. "I swear I haven't said a word about our plans. That's why I wanted you to meet her. She does this all the time," she told them, leading the way into a spacious room dedicated to comfort and clutter.

"Who's Walter?" Tish whispered as she sat in a prune-colored rocker.

Jana cleared her throat. "Her deceased husband."

Ken blinked. "De—"

"—ceased," Jana said, nodding. "Eleven years ago."

"I was supposed to tell you something," Tillie said as she plunked the teapot on the table. "It was important." She tilted her head in thought. "I distinctly remember Walter telling me not to forget. He'll be annoyed if... Ah! That's it. You're not to sign a long-term lease." She sighed in relief and darted away.

"Why not?" Ken asked her retreating back. "Why not?" he repeated as she reappeared with five cups and saucers.

"Because you'll be moving within a couple of years." Turning, she left the room again.

Laura grinned at Jana. "Does she ever sit down?"

"Eventually, when she gets everything out here."

"Why will we move?" Laura asked, as Tillie placed a bowl of brown cookies next to the teapot. Jana looked at the cookies with a puzzled frown. Bone shaped?

Tillie lifted the lid and peered at the color of the tea. "Success, dear. You'll need larger quarters."

Jana picked up a cookie and examined it. "Aunt Tillie, have you acquired a dog since my last visit?"

The older woman shook her head, continuing to pour the tea.

Tish accepted the cup. "How do you know we'll be moving?"

Bright blue eyes examined the four of them. "Walter," she said simply. "Walter said so."

And that, Laura thought, was that.

Ken absently reached for a cookie and frowned when he realized that Jana had confiscated the dish.

"Does one of your neighbors have a new puppy?" Jana persisted, accepting the cup Tillie handed her.

"How clever of you, dear. Lila—" she waved a hand to indicate the house next door "—brought home the sweetest little thing last week. Tiny, but it does have healthy lungs."

"It barks?" Jana asked.

"And cries. And howls. But how did you know?" She looked at Jana with bright eyes. "Don't tell me you can *see*! Kara does, you know. Of course, it isn't fully developed yet, but some day she'll—"

"Bite your tongue, Aunt Tillie! I cannot see, nor do I want to. My deduction was based purely on the dog biscuits." She displayed the dish. "But I don't understand what you're doing with them. Why not let Lila feed her own dog?"

Tillie examined the plate with a puzzled expression. "I could have sworn I brought out some brownies." She took the dish, did another disappearing act, then returned, offering each of them a brownie.

While they were concentrating on the chewy, nut-strewn confection, she said, "Lila's gone a lot, and I'm left with a lonely puppy practically beneath my window. So I'm teaching him to be quiet."

Four polite expressions of inquiry were directed at her.

"When he barks," she explained, "I go out and feed him. It's just a matter of retraining him, you see."

Ken wolfed down the last half of his brownie, swallowing it in one gulp. He choked on a crumb and coughed until Tish whacked him on the back and Laura handed him his tea. "It'll never work," he wheezed at Tillie. "You're doing it backward."

"He's a very clever dog," she said warmly.

Tish leaned forward. "What Ken means is that you don't reward an animal for inappropriate behavior. If you feed him when he barks, he'll think he's supposed to keep on barking."

"But—"

Jana reached out and covered her aunt's hand with her own. "You're outnumbered, Aunt Tillie. You've got a gaggle of psychologists in your living room, and any one of us can quote you paragraph, chapter and verse on behavioral changes."

"You're saying I should feed him when he isn't barking to keep him from barking?" she asked after a thoughtful pause. "I'm sure you don't mean that," she decided before any of them could respond. "If I disturbed the dog when he was quiet, he'd just howl with excitement and I'd be right back to feeding him while he was noisy. No—" she shook her head "—you must have it wrong. If I were you, I'd check those books again."

Jana grinned. Tillie had added an adopted nephew and two nieces to her immediate family that afternoon, but she had never changed her stance on behavior modification.

"Yes," she said now, looking at Tish, "tomorrow's the big day."

Tish propped her feet on the oak coffee table, crossed her ankles and leaned back in the comfortable chair. "Funny, I never thought she'd leave that house."

"I think Uncle Walter's responsible. Apparently he's been trying to get her out of La Jolla for some time. Kept telling her that there was a rambling place with tall trees waiting for her." She shrugged. "It was a fait accompli by the time I heard about it."

A worried frown wrinkled Ken's forehead. "Can she afford Rancho Santa Fe?" he asked bluntly. "It's not exactly a refuge for the middle class."

"Neither is La Jolla," Jana replied. "I suppose she can. From what I hear, this transaction was a real coup for her. Not only did she make a bundle on her old house, she got an almost new one on a prime, two-acre lot."

"Sounds too good to be true," Laura commented thoughtfully.

"I know. But the buyer is reputable, a firm that wants to build some condos on her old site. They made the original offer some time ago. Every time Aunt Tillie hesitated, they sweetened the pot. They finally bribed her with the Rancho Santa Fe property at a ridiculously low figure."

"I hope it's the right move for her," Laura said.

"Don't worry," Jana said with a grin. "I think Uncle Walter's got his finger in the pie. He'll take care of her."

"That brings up another point," Tish said.

Jana looked inquiringly at her friend.

Tish ran an agitated hand through her straight brown hair. Pink stained her cheeks, making her cool, blue eyes seem a shade deeper. "What I want to know...I mean, I don't understand... Oh, God, it sounds so stupid. Forget it.''

The three of them waited with quiet encouragement. Tish shifted uneasily, her chair creaking in the silent room. She knew they would sit there all day if they had to.

"It's Walter," she began again. "He died in that house, and Aunt Tillie stayed there all these years."

"That's right," Jana agreed, not understanding what she was leading up to.

"Well...will he know where to find her?" Tish finished in a rush.

Ken lifted her hand and planted a warm, smacking kiss in the palm. "Bless you, angel. I want to know, too. In fact, it's been driving me nuts, but I felt like an idiot asking."

Laura sighed. "Me too, guys."

Three pair of curious eyes swiveled to Jana. She cleared her throat and looked away. "Why is it I always feel like something out of the *Twilight Zone* when we talk about this? It's one thing to accept it, another entirely for four supposedly rational people to sit around discussing it." It didn't surprise her when no answer was forthcoming. She hadn't really expected one.

"All right," she admitted. "I asked." Grinning as the other three perked to attention, she said, "I have it on the best authority that Uncle Walter can find Aunt Tillie wherever and whenever he wants. Apparently neither time nor space nor distance nor anything else can keep Uncle Walter from his appointed rounds.

The next morning Jana veered off Interstate 5 and headed east on Lomas Santa Fe Drive. Slowing down as the road fed into Linea del Cielo, she breathed deeply, slowly absorbing the fragrance of citrus and eucalyptus trees. In an area known for scenic drives, this particular road, meandering past sprawling estates and stands of tall trees, was one of her favorites. It eventually led to a delightful village nestled among thousands of eucalyptus trees where she was always charmed by the rural atmosphere and some of the most interesting shops and restaurants in San Diego County.

It was odd, she thought for the hundredth time, how an unsuccessful experiment some eighty years before had contributed to the present-day charm of the area. The coming of the railroad to San Diego in the early nineteen hundreds brought with it a need for thousands of railroad ties, this in an area that got relatively little rain. And no rain, of course, meant few forests to provide wood.

Faced with this calamitous fact, the railroad officials eventually thought of a creative solution to their problem. In 1906 they bought over eight thousand acres, known as Rancho San Dieguito. They renamed it Rancho Santa Fe and planted it with three million eucalyptus seeds and seedlings. Then they waited patiently for their trees to furnish them with the necessary wood.

They had selected eucalyptus because the trees flourished in the arid climate of their native Australia. They soon learned, to their dismay, that the planted trees grew much more slowly than they had anticipated. What was even worse, the wood split so easily that it was unsuitable for railroad ties. The railroad gave up, but the magnificent groves of trees remained to shade the curving roads.

Jana slowed down, once again making appreciative noises for the unknown engineer who had deliberately designed meandering roads, forcing drivers to stick to a leisurely pace and enabling them to appreciate acacia-draped fences and lovely homes. She checked the directions Tillie had given her, mumbling, "Third street on the right after the big yellow house." Counting three streets and turning, she spotted the moving van and pulled over to the curb.

The house wasn't large and sprawling as so many of them were. It wasn't formal, multileveled or a neo-southern mansion. It was relatively small, with sparkling white stucco and a red tile roof. Jana peered through an ornate wrought iron gate at the side of the house. It led to the back garden, where a profusion of azaleas grew in shaded areas and scarlet bougainvillea draped the side fence. A latticed walkway, covered with wisteria, drew her gaze to an octagonal gazebo. White and graceful, it was a whimsical Victorian touch in the midst of early Californian. The whole effect was one of warmth and welcome. It was cozy. It was Tillie.

"Jana, dear, how long have you been here?" Tillie's greeting preceded her approach. She leaped nimbly out of the way as two men labored down the walk with a gigantic walnut armoire. "In the back bedroom," she murmured as they staggered by. The men eyed her with fascination, almost tripping over the single step leading to the porch.

Tillie had really outdone herself this morning, Jana decided. She was wearing last year's lace curtains. Or at least, it looked like it. They were held up with some gaily embroidered, red suspenders. She looked like a tipsy Bavarian milkmaid.

"Hi." Jana hugged her aunt, frowned at the two stunned movers, and the two women entered the front door. The rooms were spacious and light, the thick walls stark white. She had no doubt that Tillie's eclectic collection of wall hangings and accessories would add the necessary color and warmth. "I thought I'd beat you here."

"No, I was here at dawn." She led Jana into the kitchen. "Look at this toaster," she said proudly. "It disappears into the wall. Before the movers came I walked several miles to get acquainted with the neighborhood. It has a nice feel. Warm, harmonious." She peered into the oven. "Self-cleaning," she stated with satisfaction. "And the people seem friendly. All except that one man."

"What—"

Tillie examined an extra spigot on the sink. "Water purifier," she explained.

"—man?" Jana asked.

"The one who was washing his car. You can't imagine how irritable he was."

"Maybe it takes him a while to wake up."

"I don't think so," Tillie said slowly.

"Perhaps he hadn't had his first cup of coffee," Jana suggested. "Or maybe he just hates washing cars."

Tillie rummaged through a box and found the coffee maker. Plugging it in, she said, "He seemed nice enough at first. He smiled and we chatted."

"When did he change?"

Tillie sliced some coffee cake. "Apple," she told Jana, touching the tip of the knife to the frosted crust. "Do you think the moving men would like some?"

"When did he change?" When dealing with her aunt, Jana had learned that tact was a useless commodity. Sheer bulldog persistence was the only thing that seemed to work.

"It was... Would you like some orange juice? I have trees in the backyard. Imagine that, Jana, fresh juice from my own trees."

Jana eyed Tillie's transparent face with trepidation. Obviously she had just remembered something she wished she hadn't. "Aunt Tillie?"

Shaking her head, the older woman said, "No, that's foolish. He wouldn't be upset over such a little thing. Would he?" she appealed to Jana.

"How little?" she asked with foreboding.

"It was his car. A pretty, black one. A Mercedes. I remember because that was my second cousin's name. On my mother's side," she clarified. "Peculiar name for a car, don't you think?"

"What about the car? You didn't tell him that something's going to happen to it, did you?"

"Not exactly."

Jana groaned.

"Now, Jana, I couldn't live with myself if I didn't warn him. All he has to do is park it away from that tree and it will be all right."

"The tree," Jana repeated glumly.

"It was really a relief to know," she confided. "I've been seeing these tall trees a lot lately, even dreaming about them. Then, this morning, as I approached the man's house, Walter explained how the tree was going to fall across his driveway. And I saw it, with the little black car crushed beneath. Walter said it would happen that way. He's a very difficult man," she ended, slicing cantaloupe with unaccustomed vigor.

"Uncle Walter?" Jana asked, startled.

"The one who owns the car. He told me the tree was almost eighty years old and still healthy. That it wouldn't fall down if it was blasted with dynamite."

"And?"

"I told him I didn't know when it would happen, or how, but if he didn't find another parking place, he'd be in the market for another car."

Jana poured the coffee into mugs and carried the food to the table while Tillie rounded up the movers.

By late afternoon the furniture was in place. The two women filled bookcases, hung pictures and placed Tillie's potted plants where they would get the proper amount of sunlight. Later Jana spent the night in the guest room, listening to the driving rain of an early spring storm that caught even the weathermen by surprise.

The next morning she opened sleepy eyes and blinked in surprise at the unfamiliar pillowcase. Before she could collect her muddled thoughts, her aunt's familiar chirping whistle provided an answer to the puzzle. Tillie had an ear for music, enjoying everything from country to classical; it was unfortunate that she couldn't reproduce it. Whether she chose to whistle a Strauss waltz or soft rock, it all came out the same, sounding like a persistent but novice parakeet.

"The roof doesn't leak," Tillie announced briskly as she set a cup of coffee on the table beside Jana's bed.

"Did you expect it to?" she asked, nodding her thanks as she sat up and carefully lifted the steaming cup.

"No. I was almost sure it wouldn't, but a confirmation never hurts. The rain set some sort of a record," Tillie commented, perching at the foot of the bed. "Almost two inches last night. It hasn't rained like that since early last winter. Did you hear the wind howl?"

"Once I fell asleep, I didn't hear anything," Jana assured her. "Is it still sprinkling?"

"Oh, no. The sun is out, and it's nice and warm. I've already been for a long walk."

Jana tentatively sipped the hot coffee. "Was anything damaged?"

"Not around here," Tillie said after a careful pause.

Chapter Three

Shortly before noon the next day, Jana looked up from a case file and reached for the ringing telephone. "Jana Cantrell," she said crisply into the receiver.

"Are you free for lunch. Today?"

She recognized the deep voice immediately. How could she not? It was the only male voice that sent goose bumps sprinting down her spine; the only one that kicked up a fuss in her lungs, depriving her of the breath so necessary to sound cool and contained. She struggled with that particular vexing problem for a moment, finally managing to relocate some air and, ignoring the question, said calmly, "I was just about to call you. To set up a couple of appointments."

"Good. We'll do it at lunch. If you can make it," he prompted.

"Uh, sure. I guess so. What time?"

"Right now."

He hung up, and Jana blinked at the sound of the dial tone. Dropping the receiver softly in the cradle, she stared in frustration at the white instrument. Men! she thought in disgust, wondering how long it would take for him to travel from his office to hers. Before she had even calculated the mileage, there was a tap at the door. The telephone pealed at the same time.

"Come in," she called, reaching once again for the receiver.

Cathy's breathless voice poured into her ear. "Jana, I'm sorry. I know I'm supposed to announce your callers, but he..." It wasn't necessary to ask who *he* was; Wade stood in the doorway, his dark gaze resting on her for a moment before making a sweeping tour of the office. He reached out and absently closed the door behind him. "...just walked in and asked me to dial through to your office. He sat on the corner of my desk while he talked to you; then he smiled and thanked me, and before I could think of a thing to say he got up and went down the hall to your office," Cathy finished with a rush.

"Jana, his smile is absolutely gorgeous! *He's* gorgeous! Who is he, and how do you suppose he shaves his chin with that dimple in it?"

"Cleft," Jana murmured, staring at the chin in question. It looked stubborn, she decided.

"Is he a movie star? Do you suppose he'd autograph a picture for me?"

"I'll ask him," Jana told her, and once again cradled the receiver. She closed the folder on her desk and stood up. "My secretary wants to know if you'll autograph a picture for her."

"Of what?" he asked blankly.

"You, of course. She thinks you're a movie star."

Aside from a mutter of disgust, he remained silent.

"She also wants to know how you shave your chin," she informed him, reaching for her purse.

He rubbed it with an unconscious gesture and grinned. "Very carefully," he assured her finally. "Is she like this with everyone?"

Jana shook her head. "Only with masterful men who sit on her desk and nourish her fantasies. She'll probably never dust that corner of her desk again," she said, biting back a smile at his disconcerted expression. "If you play your cards right, she might even start a Wade Masters fan club."

"Do we have to go out that way?" Wade asked with a hunted look. "Isn't there a back door to this place?"

"You disappoint me," she mocked softly, leading him down the hall to a rear exit. "Would Charles Bronson skulk around corners? Would 007 sneak out the back door? Do you think Tom Selleck would—"

"They," he interrupted firmly, leading her to the gray car, "only outrun bullets and bombs. If they were avoiding a star struck girl barely out of high school, they'd sneak and skulk with the best of them."

Ten minutes later they were sitting at an oak table in a quiet restaurant. "Your office looks like you," Wade said suddenly, surprising himself. But the white wicker furniture with bright yellow cushions, the glass-topped desk with a bouquet of spring flowers, the colorful prints with unexpected sensual overtones, all confirmed his earlier impressions. She was a many-faceted woman, one with depth and well-concealed feelings.

Jana propped her chin on one fist, intrigued. "What did it tell you?"

"That you prefer to work in an uncluttered area. You're tolerant, warm, enjoy the absurd, dislike tension."

Jana nodded encouragement as he ticked off her various characteristics. "Perceptive man," she murmured in surprise.

"And would bring fire to a man's bed."

"What?"

"My bed," he added deliberately.

Her smile slipped at his choice of words. They matched his tone of voice and the expression in his eyes. He wasn't joking. He was, in fact, deadly serious. He was also unequivocally staking a claim.

"You've got to be kidding," she managed, wincing at her lamentable lack of originality. But it was difficult to be clever when you were confronted with a primitive man—even if he was decked out in a three-piece suit—whose thoughts ran in the direction of claims and possession.

"Not at all," he assured her. "I'm just letting you know where we're going to end up."

"In your bed?" she inquired frostily.

He nodded in casual agreement. "Or yours."

"That'll be the day," she muttered.

Jana was pleased to see that her hand didn't shake when she lifted her water glass. She wasn't sure if it was anger or shock, but something had set up a series of fine tremors throughout her body. It was one thing to react to the man, to wonder what it would feel like to be held against his muscular body, and if his voice would lower or his eyes darken when he made love. It was a whole different story to have him announce that bed was their ultimate destination. And the look in his eyes informed her that if he had anything to do with it, the journey wouldn't be a lengthy one.

His bland smile warned her that his next statement would be equally insufferable. "I told you that I like women. I especially like women who veil their passion beneath an intriguing, cool exterior."

"You make me sound like the mysterious Madame X," she said testily. "I assure you, that's not the case at all."

Wade drank his coffee, watching her over the rim of the cup.

His silent regard rattled her. With unaccustomed rashness she asked, "What makes you think I'm so passionate?"

Wade's gaze lifted politely to somewhere over her left shoulder.

"'Scuse me."

Jana looked up and met the fascinated gaze of the waitress. The woman had obviously heard the question and was breathlessly awaiting the answer. Jana felt a blush begin somewhere in the vicinity of her kneecaps and move upward. Two pairs of eyes automatically shifted to Wade. One was rounded with anticipation; the other promised mayhem if he so much as uttered a word. Only a slight compression of his lips and a quirk at the corner of his mouth betrayed him.

"More coffee?"

Wade nodded to the waitress. "Please." As soon as she was out of earshot, he continued, "Because I'm a man and I'm not blind. Your walk, your talk, the expression in your eyes—everything about you gives it away. Don't you think you are?''

A good question, Jana admitted to herself. It deserved a good answer. The only problem was, she didn't have one. She knew she was affectionate, even loving—but passionate? She simply didn't know, hadn't had the opportunity to find out. She had been reared in the midst of a loving family that had taught her the value of self-esteem and to equate sex with commitment; it was, she'd learned, not a commodity to be lightly given or shared. Sometimes she wondered if those values weren't as extinct as the dodo, but even if they were, she was stuck with them.

Up to now, it hadn't seemed like such a disadvantage. But, looking at the man across from her, she realized that things were getting complicated. He had decided she was passionate. Had he also concluded that she was experienced? Probably. She gave a depressed sigh.

''Are we here to talk business or so you can tell me how great we'd be in bed?'' she demanded. Too late, she saw an arm extended over her shoulder, a hand holding the coffee pot. Jana looked up at the goggle-eyed waitress. She sighed. At this rate the woman was going to pull up a chair and join them so she wouldn't miss the next episode.

Wade calmly thanked the waitress and received an adoring glance in return. It reminded Jana of the way the women scattered around the room had stared as he led the way to their table. The man definitely had something. Eyeing him consideringly, Jana decided that it was an aura of maleness. He wasn't handsome in the classical or contemporary sense, but just looking at him made a woman aware of her femininity and left her rejoicing in it. It wasn't fair, she decided. Considering her lack of experience with . . . what was the male equivalent of a femme fatale? she wondered. Well, whatever it was, it just wasn't fair to pit her against one. She had survived almost twenty-seven years without the experience, so why, at this point in her life, did fate seem to think it was necessary?

The waitress departed with a final wistful look over her shoulder. Jana breathed a sigh of relief and decided it was time to change the subject. "You look like you got locked up with a cage full of cats over the weekend," she commented, pointing to his scratched hands.

"Feels that way, too," he admitted. "The storm knocked over a tree on my property, and I spent most of yesterday with a chain saw clearing up the mess." He bit into his ham sandwich and chewed reflectively. "It almost got my car. If I hadn't moved it, it would have been buried under a ton or so of tree."

Jana felt a cold spot on her nape that quickly trickled down her back. This time it had nothing to do with Wade's voice. She had become familiar with this particular sensation during the last year. The first time it had happened was when one of Aunt Tillie's predicted disasters had occurred; the last time was when her friend had been unable to dodge the little red car. Now she was remembering the peculiar tone of Tillie's voice the morning before. "Not around here," she had said.

If not there, then where? A mile or so away? At a house where a stubborn man washed his car and refused to believe that a tree would fall on it? No, she groaned silently, anything but that. How could she work with the man if Aunt Tillie was going to drop trees—and God only knew what else—on him?

"Was it the gray car we came in?" she asked at last.

Wade shook his head, unknowingly sounding the death knell to her hopes. "A black Mercedes. Funny thing about that." He took another bite, chewed and swallowed.

"Oh?" she asked in a hollow voice.

"I was out early Saturday morning washing it, and a little woman in strange clothes popped up from out of nowhere and told me I should move it."

"That is funny," she agreed absently, wondering if she should confess all and plead for mercy, or remain silent and hope for the best.

Wade's gaze sharpened at her abstracted tone. "No, the funny part is, she told me the tree would fall on it if I didn't get it out of the way."

"Ah." Jana nodded and stopped at that. It seemed like a nice, safe, encouraging sound.

"I told her that the tree had been around for a lot of years and I didn't think it was going to topple over."

"Ummm."

"She just smiled, suggested that I move it and disappeared. I almost left it there."

"Oh?"

His smile was wry. "Just out of sheer stubbornness. But I couldn't get it out of my mind, so the last thing I did on Saturday night was pull it into the garage."

Jana thought he was through and reached for her cup. It fell into the saucer with a clatter when he added, "I thought I saw her yesterday morning, but by the time I got around the tree, she was gone."

"Really?" she croaked. Being evasive is damn hard work, she decided, wondering if she dared reach for her water.

"I'd like to talk to her."

Jana's brows rose in surprise. "Why?"

"At first, I thought she was a crackpot—"

You'd be surprised at the number of people who might agree with you, Aunt Tillie's niece commented silently.

"—but now I think she might be psychic."

"And you actually want to meet her?"

"The subject fascinates me," he admitted.

"An academic interest is one thing, but being around someone like that could be nerveracking," Jana commented idly.

"How so?"

"What if she predicted something else? Just suppose you were going on a business trip and she had bad vibes about the plane you were scheduled to use. Would you cancel your reservations? Or would you get on the plane and develop a bleeding ulcer waiting for it to crash into a mountain? What if she said another tree was going to fall? Would you believe her?"

"I don't know. I'd like the chance to find out, though," he said finally. "She might even be able to tell me when you'll fall into my bed," he added with a grin.

Jana's eyes glistened with gold flecks of humor at the thought. "That might be a bit out of her realm."

"Oh?"

She nodded. "I don't know that a psychic would clutter up her circuits estimating when my passionate body will join yours in bed." Jana saw a flicker of amusement cross his face and knew she had done it again. She looked up with resignation and met the speculative gaze of the waitress.

"You folks want any dessert?" Her envious tone indicated that she expected to be trampled as they rushed out the door for an afternoon of lusty pleasure.

Jana shook her head. Her "no" was a strangled whisper. "For heaven's sake," she muttered to Wade, "will you please ask her for the bill and get us out of here?"

Much later she realized that once again she had forgotten to confirm the appointments with Wade.

A week passed, punctuated with daily reminders of Wade, ranging from a pink rosebud in a vase to an extra-large pizza with pepperoni, personally delivered to, and shared in, her office. There were also strange, abstracted calls from Aunt Tillie. On the one hand, she felt pursued by an equable but marauding wolf; on the other, despite her efforts, Tillie seemed to be deliberately drifting away.

Friday evening Jana reached for the telephone, determined to question her elusive aunt. She had learned over the past year that Tillie was perfectly coherent and logical...unless she was disturbed about something. And when she was, she was as hard to pin down as a greased pig. Poking at the numbers, she settled back to wait. It was answered on the second ring.

"Hello, Jana. How are you, dear?"

"Fine, Aunt Tillie." It had taken a while, Jana remembered, but it no longer alarmed her when her aunt answered the telephone that way. "The question is, how are *you*?" Kara had taught her to be direct when dealing with their mutual aunt. Tillie was incapable of lying, but she was a past master at changing the subject.

"Busy, dear, busy. So many things to do, what with a new house and all."

"Aunt Tillie—"

"Shopping, and working in the garden...and I painted the front door red to match the roof."

"Aunt Tillie—"

"You'll love the Chinese gong I found at a garage sale."

"Aunt—*gong?*"

"It makes such a delicious, clangy noise. Every time I hear it, I expect Yul Brynner to come through the door."

"Yul—"

"The King of Siam, you know."

"Aunt—"

"I've been using the gazebo. It's so peaceful—most of the time."

"*Tillie!*"

"You needn't shout, dear. My hearing is quite good."

Jana rubbed at the crease forming between her brows. She was going to be old and wrinkled before her time. One more thing to thank Kara for. Grasping at her aunt's last statement, she said, "Tell me about the gazebo."

"It means 'a gazing place,' you know."

"And now that the weather's warm, you're sitting out there," Jana encouraged quietly.

"It's so lovely. The flowers are so fragrant." Tillie's voice was softly reflective. "The bees and hummingbirds love them. I use it to meditate. And to discuss things with Walter."

"Uh, how's he doing?" Jana asked, stumbling a bit as she inquired about the deceased man, but wondering if somehow he was the problem. The silence that followed convinced her that she was on the right track.

"I'm quite put out with Walter," Tillie stated.

"What's he done?" Jana asked in surprise. "I didn't think that anyone where he ... is got into trouble," she finished awkwardly. She wished for the hundredth time that she could figure out how to mention the man without sounding like an absolute fool.

Tillie's anger hummed over the wires. "He deceived me."

"Are you sure?" Jana blinked in bewilderment. Another woman? And if so, how on earth had Tillie found out? Unless he was fool enough to confess. That wasn't impossible, of course. God only knew the man was talkative enough. But how had he ever managed something of that nature where he was? Jana's vague visions of halos, puffy clouds, benevolent smiles and angel wings suffered a distinct setback.

"He didn't tell me the truth."

Jana sighed with relief. Well, good for him. At least he had *some* sense. Although she still didn't understand ...

"I suppose I should say he just told me part of it," Tillie clarified. "What you would call a sin of omission. But that doen't mean I'm not angry."

Jana felt a familiar sense of bafflement wash over her. She was a psychologist, she reminded herself. She was *trained* to talk to people, to draw them out, to help them verbalize their thoughts. Why was it that one small woman could defeat her? Perhaps, a small voice leaped to her defense, because Tillie's conversation did not follow anything approaching a normal pattern. There was no straight line with a few lapses into wiggles and wobbles. She tended to meander in circles. No, the voice decided after a moment's reflection, Tillie definitely followed a corkscrew pattern.

"I think I've missed something," Jana confessed. "What are we talking about?"

"Haven't you been listening? The house, Jana, the house."

Swallowing the comment that was on the tip of her tongue, she asked, "Don't you like it?"

"I love it," her aunt answered promptly.

Jana propped her bare feet on the coffee table and stared at her toes. This woman was going to drive her *nuts*. "Does the roof leak?"

"Of course not. I told you the day after the storm that it didn't. Remember?"

"Oh, yeah. Is there something wrong with the garden?"

"It's perfect," Tillie said with enthusiasm.

"How about the gazebo?" By now, Jana was frankly grasping at straws. The extended silence alerted her. "Aunt Tillie, does something bother you when you use the gazebo?" More silence. "Do you see things out there?"

"Trees," she burst out. "It's always the eucalyptus trees. And now I know why. But Walter should have told me."

"What's the matter, love?" Jana asked softly. "Are you worried about them falling? We can have some-one check to see if they're healthy."

"I saw them long before I ever saw the house," Tillie said. "I thought it was Walter's way of showing me where I would be living. Once the house was in es-crow, I thought they would go away, but I still keep seeing them. When the tree fell in that man's yard—and isn't it a good thing he moved his car?—I thought that would be the end of it. But I still kept seeing them. Now I know why."

"Why?" Jana asked reasonably.

"Because of the view from the gazebo." Tillie's pa-tient tone implied that she had gone through this once, but she would repeat it, slowly if necessary, for her backward niece.

"You don't like seeing the trees," Jana said slowly, feeling as if she were stumbling blindfolded along a mountain path.

"I love the trees," her contrary aunt claimed. "They're stately, graceful and seem as old as time. They give me a feeling of permanence, of continu-ity."

"Then what—"

"What I'm having trouble with is the bodies."

Chapter Four

*B*odies? Jana threw some clothes in an overnight bag, turned off the lights, locked the windows and doors, and dashed for her car. How could anyone, she wondered, even Aunt Tillie, say a cheerful good-night and hang up after dropping a bombshell like that? After maneuvering the car out of the cul de sac, one of the many in the planned community of stylish town houses, she waved to the guard at the security gate and headed for the freeway. Her brow wrinkled in a frown of concentration, she recalled the rest of the conversation.

"Bodies? Is that what you said? No, of course it isn't," she had said, interrupting herself, certain she was mistaken, but unable to think of anything that sounded similar.

"Bodies," Tillie repeated calmly. "Swinging from the trees."

"Dead?"

Tillie was shocked. "Of course not. If that were the case I would have notified the police. But I'll tell you all about it the next time you visit. Good night, Jana, dear. Thank you for calling."

And that had been that. Before she could open her mouth, she was listening to the dial tone. And Tillie was no doubt humming contentedly, getting ready for bed, little knowing or caring that her niece was still sitting, staring at a wall, holding the buzzing telephone to her ear.

Twenty minutes later Jana was pulling up before the white stucco house. Turning off the ignition, she eyed the house with surprise. She had driven in a thoughtful haze, automatically passing the eleven hundred acres of Balboa Park, the cities of La Jolla and Del Mar, and winding up the curving roads to the house. That was either very good or very bad driving, she thought, and immediately wondered which. Noting that the lights were still on in the house, she tugged at her overnight case and slammed the car door, deciding that a critique of her driving skills could wait until later.

Jana pressed the doorbell and waited. It wasn't long before she heard rustling from inside the house. She used to worry about Tillie's habit of throwing open the door, until Kara had reminded her that their aunt had no use for peepholes or cautious inquiries. She always knew who was waiting to be admitted.

"Jana, dear, how nice to see you. Did you tell me you were coming for a visit?" Tillie greeted her calmly, with only a hint of perplexity.

Jana leaned forward and kissed her aunt noisily on the cheek. "No, my favorite aunt, I did not. And the reason I didn't was because you hung up on me."

"How rude of me," Tillie murmured absently, ushering Jana through to the yellow and white bedroom reserved for her. "Why did I do that?"

Jana eased her case onto the airy print comforter that served as a bedspread. "Possibly because you didn't want to tell me any more about the you-know-whats swinging from the you-know-wheres."

Tillie's bright blue gaze met Jana's hazel one. "No, that wasn't why," she said slowly, remembering. "I meant to have a long talk with Walter. Thank you for reminding me." She reached up to kiss Jana's cheek. "I'll go do that right now. Sleep well, dear. I'll see you in the morning."

Jana watched the door close with a familiar blend of affection and exasperation. It wouldn't do a bit of good to go after her. Tillie had been wearing her determined look; she wouldn't forget her mission this time. Sighing philosophically, Jana emptied her case. At least she was here on the premises, and no bodies—no visible ones, she amended silently—were floating around. The best thing to do, she informed herself, was to get a good night's sleep. She had the feeling she'd need her strength to face the next day. Whatever it brought, it was bound to be troublesome, and far from ordinary. After closing the white eyelet curtains she undressed, dropped a shorty nightgown over her head and crawled in bed.

Later a drowsy chuckle sounded in the dark room. She'd give a lot to be a fly on the wall while Aunt Tillie tore into Uncle Walter.

Jana jerked upright, still half-asleep, her eyes wide open. Sunlight poured through the curtains, birds in the orange trees were noisily practicing a symphony, and a God-awful explosion of tinny vibrations resounded through the room. She stared at the open door, fully expecting to see Genghis Khan and his entire army sweep through.

"What do you think?" Tillie's voice preceded her through the door. "That's the gong I told you about. Isn't it marvelous? It's on a stand with wheels so you can take it almost anywhere, and there's a funny, padded stick attached to beat it with. I love to begin the day with one good whack."

Jana bit back a giggle. Tillie's face was alight with enthusiasm, and she was dragging the gong behind her. She was wearing a bright pink kimono snugly belted high on her ribcage. The silky material formed a network of pleats that swelled, gaining fullness, until it fell to her ankles with the illusion of being draped over a hoop skirt.

She beamed at Jana's appreciative expression. "I knew you'd like it. Isn't it a perfect way to celebrate the dawn of a new day?"

"Perfect," Jana agreed. The smile faded as a surge of love washed over her for the childlike spirit of her aunt. Not childish, she thought, making the distinction, just filled with the pure love of adventure and discovery that a child too soon outgrew. But Tillie had retained it; it was the part of her that appreciated the unique quality of each growing plant and cherished the small daily incidents that so enriched life.

Tillie rolled the gong into a corner and gave it an absentminded pat. "Breakfast is ready. Come and see how lovely the garden is this morning."

Jana washed quickly, combed her hair, made the bed and joined Tillie in the kitchen. "Did you, ah, talk things over with Uncle Walter last night?"

Tillie poured milk on her cereal. Looking earnestly at Jana, she said, "I misjudged Walter. He's taking care of me just as he always has." She crunched on a piece of toast as if the subject had been sufficiently dealt with.

"But, what about the—" Jana stopped abruptly. Over cereal, toast and orange juice, and with the sunlight warm on a bouquet of roses in the center of the table, it seemed absurd to be discussing bodies— swinging, warm, or any other kind. "You know," she ended weakly.

Tillie set down her coffee cup. "Oh, that." She waved one hand in a vague gesture. "Walter said it would all work out and I'm not to worry about it." She took her dishes over to the sink and rinsed them.

Jana's frowning gaze followed her. And who, she wondered grimly, is going to take care of it so it all works out? She had the depressing conviction that she was elected. "Will you at least tell me what the problem is?" she asked quietly.

Tillie peered out the window. "There's Mr. Franks. He can tell you all about it. My neighbor," she amplified, as Jana joined her to watch the tall, bald man moving around his garden. "He's the one who explained it to me. Nice man," she added. "But he has strange habits. He plants worms," she said darkly before leaving the room.

Jana entered the shady latticed walkway, touching the clusters of white and lavender wisteria before stepping into the sunny garden. Following a brick walk past the gazebo, she called, "Mr. Franks?" to the man bending over a brilliant red rosebush. She watched him straighten and turn, and found herself being sized up by intelligent gray eyes.

"Yes."

She introduced herself. "Aunt Tillie is upset about something and said you could explain it."

He gave a snort of disgust. "She's in good company. We're all chewing nails over this thing." His baritone voice was clipped with anger. "I've already called my lawyer and discussed it."

Wishing that someone, anyone, would start at the beginning and discuss it with her, Jana said, "I'm afraid you're going too fast for me. I don't even know what's happening."

After another sharp glance, he gestured to an umbrella-covered patio table. "Let's get in the shade; this will take awhile." After they were seated, he said, "It's the property back there." His sweeping wave seemed to cover a lot of ground. "Or, I should say, the people on it." He looked at her mystified expression and sighed. "I'm not making a lot of sense, am I?"

Jana's smile matched his. "Mr. Franks—"

"Glen, Jana. Look." He pulled a pencil and pad from his shirt pocket and rapidly sketched something that resembled a patchwork quilt. "This is your aunt's property, here's mine, the Simmonses', Raleys', Greenes' and Ferrelis', roughly in the shape of a chevron. The wedge-shaped piece that fits in the middle, adjoining all our lots at one place or another, belongs to Mrs. Benjamin, known to one and all as Benny. She's the problem."

Jana felt as if her face was one big question mark.

"It used to belong to old Eli Benjamin. When he died, he left it to his son. Before probate was completed, *he* died. We ended up with Benny as a neighbor. I have nothing against her personally, but she's strange."

Jana wondered fleetingly what *she* planted. Bodies, probably. "How strange?"

"Very. She's one of these way-out psychologists and she holds seminars on her property."

"Psychologist?" she queried, as if she had never heard the word. "What kind of seminars?"

"Some kind of confidence-building thing," he said vaguely.

"There really is a need for groups like that," she pointed out.

His gray eyes gleamed with determination. "There may be, but not the way she does it. And not behind my property."

"What exactly does she do?"

"Damned if I know what goes on inside. The outside monkeyshines are driving us all crazy, though."

"Like what?" she asked patiently, wondering if she was ever going to find out.

"Like swinging from the eucalyptus trees, yodeling like Tarzan."

"I beg your pardon?"

He smiled grimly at her stunned expression. "You don't believe me," he stated. "Can't say that I blame you. Hell, I didn't believe it at first and I *saw* it. Come here a minute." He led her back beyond the garden into the south forty and pointed to a row of tall trees. "See those?" At her nod, he continued. "They run more or less along our mutual boundary lines. From there to there," he gestured, "is your aunt's property. Mine runs to that point, then the Simmonses'—"

"—Raleys', Greenes' and Ferrelis'," Jana finished with him. "How close to the property lines are the trees?"

"Too damn close. You notice that none of us have fences. Never had any need for them, but I'm thinking about getting one that's twenty feet high and soundproof."

"It's that bad?"

"Worse. If you stick around, you'll see what I mean. See the ladder, thick rope and platform on that tree? Benny put them on every blasted tree that follows the boundary line. I think the crazies in her group graduate when they make it from one tree to the next, following the elongated circle back to her house."

"Wait a minute. I don't understand how the rope thing works."

"It's tied to a thick branch of the first tree. Someone swings on it to the second tree. If he doesn't make it, he slides down, grabs the end of the rope and walks it back so the next one can try."

"If he does make it?"

He shrugged. "I guess the next person reverses the order and swings from the second back to the first. Mostly, at least at first, no one makes it. Tillie can be grateful that those smaller acacias," he waved at a mass of tangled limbs heavy with yellow blossoms, "block out part of the obstacle course. God knows she needs every bit of help she can get," he finished heavily.

"What do you mean?" she asked, and wished she hadn't, as his brow shot up.

"Because she gets the brunt of it. That's the starting point, where each and every one of them begins. Swinging and yelling. The neophytes usually drop like flies off the first tree. It takes them a while to get started. Not long enough, though," he added gloomily. "As they get more confident, they start yowling and going farther."

"But this is a residential area," she protested. "How can she get away with such shenanigans?"

"That's exactly what we're asking," he replied grimly.

"What's being done about it?"

"We've all gone over there and raised hell. We started with discussion, moved on to threats and finally turned to our lawyers. She's a stubborn woman. Won't listen to a thing we say."

"What do the lawyers say?"

"That they're looking into it," he said disgustedly. "And they periodically remind us that the legal process is neither swift nor inexpensive."

Jana followed him back to the table. "It doesn't sound very encouraging."

"You can say that again, in spades. But we're not giving up. We've lived in this area a long time, moved here because of its rural atmosphere. We want it to stay that way. We'll think of something to quiet them down."

Jana looked at his determined face and believed him. "I'm glad I'm on your side," she said with a smile. "Let me know if I can do anything." She started down the walk and turned back. "Oh, Glen, Aunt Tillie mentioned your worms. Is it a state secret, or can you tell me what you do with them?"

He grinned. "Nothing sinister. I'm a fisherman. They're nightcrawlers. For bait." Her gurgle of amusement broadened his smile.

"Well, that's one mystery solved, anyway. See you later." Walking away, she spotted Tillie pulling the few weeds that had managed to find their way into the rose garden. She called out that she was going for a walk and waved as the older woman nodded.

A couple of hours and several miles later, she stopped in confusion. She had started out with no destination in mind, simply wandering up one street and down another, and had lost all sense of direction. Of course, that wasn't hard to do in this neighborhood, she reminded herself. There didn't seem to be one straight street in the entire city. If there was, she certainly hadn't found it. Besides, her attention had been on gorgeous homes, manicured lawns and bountiful beds of flowers, not on street signs.

The quiet hum of an engine caught her attention. A sleek gray car was keeping pace with her. It stopped when she did.

Wade leaned over and opened the passenger door. "Hop in. What are you doing in my neck of the woods?"

Jana scooted in and slammed the door. She took one look at the dark eyes devouring her and almost jumped back out. "I'm trying to find my way out of the maze," she said lightly. "I not only don't know where I am, I haven't the foggiest idea how to get where I want to go."

"The first one is simple," he said, putting the car in gear. "You're five houses away from my place. Come have a cool drink with me and we'll work on the second one."

She watched with interest as he pulled into the driveway of a rambling pale yellow house with a shake roof. Strategically placed ferns spread their luxuriant, lacy fronds along the front. A large weeping willow was reflected in the sparkling windows.

"So what are you doing up here?" he repeated as he inserted the key and opened the front door.

"Visiting my aunt," she replied absentmindedly as she looked around. The room was large, very large. It was also warm and welcoming, with earth-toned, comfortable furniture, green plants and lots of light. A large hand on her back lightly directed her over gleaming wood floors to the kitchen. This is the way I would furnish a home if I had unlimited funds and the time to shop around, she decided.

"What'll it be?" Wade asked, opening the refrigerator. "Anything from diet drinks to hard stuff, with juice, tea and coffee in between."

"Diet cola," she opted, and waited patiently as he dropped ice cubes in a tall glass.

He poured the drink and led her outside to a long, redwood deck overlooking a pool. "You don't look like you need that stuff," he commented, eyeing her trim waist and flaring hips.

Jana smiled wryly and sat on an old-fashioned porch swing. "I love to eat and I hate to exercise, so I need all the help I can get. This is a beautiful house," she said, not bothering to be subtle about changing the subject.

"Yeah," he replied absently, sitting beside her, his mind obviously not on the structure in question.

She wiggled uncomfortably. "I wish you'd stop that. You're looking at me like a man dying of thirst would eye a jug of water."

"I know. That's just about the way I feel. You're a beautiful woman," he said.

"I've been accused of a lot of things," Jana said with a grin, determined to keep things light, "but never of being beautiful."

"Take my word for it." He leaned forward and his thigh touched hers.

Jana looked up just as he bent his head and dropped a kiss on her soft lips. Her eyes widened in surprise, then closed. Her blood seemed to warm up about ten degrees, making her skin prickle. Hold on, girl, she told herself. It was just a kiss, nothing to get excited about. Her hazel gaze rose to meet his brown one, and she changed her mind. Forget excited, she decided; try worried, anxious and full of trepidation. She wondered if it was too late to pretend that he hadn't affected her and decided it was. The ice cubes chattering against the side of her glass would tell a blind man, and his vision, like a number of other things, was perfect.

Shifting slightly, she returned to the last safe topic she could remember. "Your pool is lovely."

"Um-hmm. You're going to have to give me a list of forbidden subjects. I seem to bring one up every time I open my mouth."

She slanted a look up at him. "You're a stubborn man."

"Um-hmm. You don't want to talk about how passionate you are, or how long it will be before we go to—"

"And difficult."

"—bed, or how beautiful you are. What's left?"

"There are all sorts of things," she pointed out. "My job, your job—"

"Dull," he said with a slow smile.

"—and," she said with quiet deliberation, "my psychic aunt who knows when trees are going to fall on pretty black cars."

"Very du—*what?*" He glared down at her. "You mean that little woman in the funny clothes belongs to you? And you didn't say anything?"

Jana bit back a satisfied smile. All thoughts of seduction had been swept out of his mind, at least for the moment. In fact, if his expression was anything to go by, she could dance nude on his patio table and all he'd do was ask for Tillie's address. Her eyes narrowed in thought. Obviously she would have to introduce them now. But it had been inevitable—with only the timing in question—from the moment Tillie moved into his neighborhood. And if diverting his attention worked to her own advantage, so much the better.

"When can I meet her?"

"Is today soon enough?"

"Right now? Let's go."

Jana grinned at his eagerness. Gone was the business tycoon, the wolf on the prowl. He was more like a boy being taken to see a magician. "Do you mind if I call her first, to see if it's okay?"

"Oh. Sure." He visibly restrained himself. "The telephone's in the kitchen. I'll come with you."

She dialed while Wade hovered over her. Tillie answered on the ninth ring.

"Hello, Jana. What a perfect time to call. I've been visiting my neighbors and I just walked in."

"Mr. Franks?"

"No. On the other side. Mrs. Whatshername. Benny. And her guests. They're perfectly delightful. When are you bringing your friend over?"

"I don't know why, after all this time, I'm still surprised when you do that," Jana wondered aloud.

"Because it hasn't happened to you . . . yet."

"Don't even think it. Be satisfied that you've passed it on to one niece."

"Tell your young man that I'm glad his car wasn't damaged. Do you think he'd enjoy an early dinner in the gazebo? It's such a lovely day, we shouldn't waste it by eating inside."

"Just a minute." She raised her eyes to Wade's impatient ones. "Can you come for dinner? Early?" At his pleased nod, she raised the receiver to her mouth. "Okay, but don't go to any trouble. Let's make it a picnic, and we'll supply the food. See you later."

"Sorry 'bout that," she said to Wade as she replaced the telephone and turned to him. "Aunt Tillie's cooking is erratic at the best of times. On spur of the moment occasions it's impossible. If we don't pick up something, you might end up with orange juice from her trees and lots of conversation."

"No problem." He glanced at his watch. "What time?"

"About three. She usually catnaps in the afternoon."

"So we've got several hours. Are you hungry?"

She nodded. "Starved."

"How about having lunch at The Inn?" He enjoyed the look of quick pleasure that filled her eyes.

"I'd love it. I've walked around the grounds, but I've never been there at the right time for a meal." As they got in his car, she had a sudden thought. "Now that I know someone who lives here, do I get to join the locals and call it 'The Inn'?"

"You have my permission," he assured her.

She'd have to bring Tillie someday, she decided, as they pulled into the parking lot.

The Inn at Rancho Santa Fe had been built by the Santa Fe Railroad in the early twenties and was one of her favorite places. The original guesthouse, constructed of adobe dug from the site, was now part of the main building. Situated on the knoll of a hill, it was surrounded by charming guest cottages scattered through twenty acres of beautiful woods and landscaped grounds.

Once they were seated in the garden room, overlooking the sparkling pool, Wade wasted no time. "Tell me all about your aunt."

"That's a big order," she murmured from behind the menu.

He contained himself until they gave their orders to the waitress. "So what does she do besides wear...ah, interesting clothes and give warnings?"

"She worries about her gift. She's a warm, delightful person, and I love her very much," Jana said coolly, giving a warning of her own.

"Sorry." He laced his fingers with hers until their palms met. "The whole thing fascinates me, but I didn't mean to sound flippant."

"I know." Her eyes held his. "Aunt Tillie sees the good in everyone and probably wouldn't recognize a put-down if it walked up and introduced itself." She was silent for a long moment, but finally said, "I just realized that she seems to bring out the best in everyone. Regardless of what people think, they're always kind to her. But, still, I tend to be a mite overprotective."

He accepted that and moved on to his next question. "Why didn't you tell her who you were bringing over?"

"I didn't have to," she explained, amusement lighting her eyes. "She told me." His brows shot up, and she complacently picked at her salad.

"Does she do that often?" His curiosity was genuine.

"Most of the time," she admitted. "Aunt Tillie is usually 'on,' in touch with that extra sense." When he remained silent for several moments, she asked, "Does that bother you?"

"No. I was just remembering what you said that day in the restaurant."

"You mean the day I was suffering from foot-in-mouth disease? What did I say worth remembering?"

"Something about it being nerveracking to be around a psychic. I didn't realize that you were speaking from experience."

"You weren't meant to."

"Has she ever seen anything upsetting about you?"

Jana shook her head and raised crossed fingers. "Not yet. I live a fairly placid life. But last year, when Tijuana had that bad earthquake, my cousin was visiting down there and got hurt. Aunt Tillie knew. The hellish thing is, she rarely sees the whole picture. She knew that Kara had a head injury, but not if she was dead or alive."

"Tough," he sympathized. "Why did she decide to move to this area?" he asked, as much out of curiosity as to bring back her smile.

Unwilling to introduce Uncle Walter just yet, Jana took a bite of salad and thought about the question. "Someone suggested that she look in the area," she said finally.

Wade nodded in understanding. "Her financial adviser?"

"You might say that," Jana said with a straight face.

"Did I say something funny?"

"Not a thing."

"Then you might try wiping that grin off your face." Her mouth grew solemn, but her green-flecked eyes laughed at him. It amazed him how much he enjoyed sitting across the table from this vibrant, laughing girl-woman. The hunger that curled through his body, stirring tendrils of warmth and tension, amazed him even more. He couldn't remember ever wanting a woman as badly as he wanted this one. And he had *never* needed one.

Jana studied Wade Masters and reminded herself that she had obligations—to her partners and the clinic. She really couldn't afford to be diverted from the master plan. And this man could definitely be a diversion—more than that—a major complication. She tried to ignore the voice that reminded her that she also had an obligation to herself. All right, all right, she capitulated. I'll take time for myself...soon. In the meantime there was no harm in introducing a business acquaintance to her aunt. Was there?

Chapter Five

We're back, Aunt Tillie," Jana called, stepping behind Wade to close the door. His arms were full of bags holding steaming fried chicken and all the trimmings. She put her hand between his shoulder blades and nudged him in the direction of the kitchen, watching her feet as they moved because she couldn't see anything besides his broad back and the massive stretch of his shoulders. She wondered if he could possibly still be growing. "I'm sorry if we're late."

Tillie's serene voice floated back from the kitchen. "No, there's more than enough time. I'm making some coffee. It's still warm outside. That line at the chicken place was wretched, wasn't it?"

Wade stopped dead in his tracks, and Jana slammed into him. He looked down at her with wide eyes. "How did she—"

Jana bit back a smile at his reaction. If she was lucky, she might witness the imperturbable Mr. Masters lose his cool. "You wanted to see a psychic in action, didn't you? Now's your chance." She reached out to rescue a slipping carton. "Here, let me take that."

They dumped the bags on the bar and turned to Tillie. Wade stared in fascination at his hostess. Her silver curls had rebelled against any form of control and her dress was a drifty sort of thing in a blinding shade of blue. He blinked and held out his hand as Jana introduced them.

Tillie returned his smile with a brilliant one of her own and captured his hand between both of hers, patting it. "You've taken your time, but you'll do very well," she said thoughtfully before turning away. Her gaze rested momentarily on her niece. "I think your master plan is in jeopardy," she commented thoughtfully.

Wade wondered what it was about the enigmatic statement that rooted Jana to the floor and stained her cheeks with pink. Before he could decide, his attention was drawn back to Tillie.

"This neighborhood seems quite safe," she told him, watching the level of coffee rise in the pot, "but it's a bad habit to leave your keys in the ignition."

He patted his pockets with an automatic gesture. "I never—"

"You did this time," she assured him gently.

He checked his pockets again, even the one in his shirt, before muttering something beneath his breath and heading for the front door. He was back within seconds. "You were right," he admitted.

"Yes," she said without surprise, "I usually am." Her head tilted as she surveyed him. "I don't understand about your work. I see a computer and your office—and how you work in that clutter is beyond me—but I don't understand what the eyes are."

Wade's eyes involuntarily sought Jana's, and she held up her hands in a gesture of surrender. "Don't look at me; I'm innocent," she declared. "I never said a word."

He nodded at Tillie. "Photoelectric cells," he verified. At her baffled look, he continued. "It's a cell whose electrical state is changed by the effect of light. It's usually incorporated in an electric circuit and used in mechanical devices. It's also," he added softly, "usually called an electric eye." Her eyes met his, brightening with an expression of dawning satisfaction. She hadn't fathomed a word he'd uttered, he realized, but at least now the "eyes" made sense.

As she turned away and briskly directed her niece to put the silverware and napkins in a basket, he could see the strong bond of affection between them. Jana, he knew, would hover over her aunt with the fierceness of a guard dog. And if he spent much time around this fey, enchanting little woman, he thought with a smile, he'd be right there beside her. He shook his head and voiced a mild complaint. "Am I the only one who's hungry? I could eat the hind leg of a horse."

"The gazebo is a perfect place for a picnic meal," Jana said as they sat down at the linen-covered table. "I'm glad you suggested it."

Tillie looked around with a satisfied air. "It is nice, isn't it? Walter likes it, too."

Wade stopped serving potato salad long enough to look up. "Walter?"

"My husband."

"That's right." Wade glanced at Jana. "You mentioned your uncle to me."

Jana nodded, not looking up from the messy job of buttering her corn on the cob.

"How much time I wasted," Tillie said, sighing. "Two years ago Walter suggested moving out here. If I had known how nice it was going to be, I wouldn't have delayed."

"He's your financial adviser, isn't he?" Wade asked, slowly piecing bits of conversation together.

"Yes." Tillie nibbled at a chicken leg. "And he certainly keeps me busy, selling off this stock and buying that one."

"Why doesn't he do it himself?" Wade asked reasonably.

"I wish he could," Tillie admitted. "But not everyone listens to Walter."

Jana stoically kept her eyes on her corn, methodically eating her way through two rows at a time, twisting the cob a notch before beginning on the next section of golden kernels.

Wade frowned. "Then he should change his stockbroker."

"I mentioned that to him once, but he said not to."

"I'd never do business with a man who didn't listen to me."

Tillie tilted her head thoughtfully. "You do have a certain advantage," she murmured. "Oh dear, I forgot to bring lemon for the tea. Excuse me a moment.''

Wade looked after her, then at Jana. "I'll bite. What's my advantage. Youth?"

"Life," she enunciated clearly.

He eyed her as if she had just sprouted another head. "You don't mean that he's . . ."

She nodded. "Deceased."

Wade dropped his chicken. "*Dead?* As in appearing in the obituary column and having a funeral?"

Jana nodded again.

His voice was hushed as he looked back at the house. "Does she know?"

She thought carefully before answering. "Yes. Rationally, that is. But she believes in life after life. Therefore, he's alive. Maybe not here, but somewhere."

"When?"

Jana sighed. This was every bit as hard as she had thought it would be. "Eleven years ago."

"But she said that two years ago he wanted her to move."

"That's right. And yesterday he told her something else. And tomorrow, he'll be—"

"Oh my God, are you telling me that he . . ."

"Talks to her?" She nodded judiciously. "Yes, that's a fair description."

Wade picked up his chicken leg, regarded it speculatively and put it aside. His face was carefully expressionless as he poked at the salad.

"Here we are." Tillie set the dish of sliced lemons on the table. "You're not eating," she said in concern, examining Wade's plate. "Here, have another piece of chicken."

"I've still got this one," he pointed out.

She looked at the spread of his shoulders. "You're a big man. You need a lot of food. Take some more," she urged.

He nodded his thanks, then froze with his hand outstretched, staring over her shoulder.

Jana's quick glance encompassed his narrowed eyes and rigid posture. Hastily she followed the direction of his gaze. "What's the matter?" she whispered.

"I thought I saw—never mind," he muttered, absently biting into a buttered roll. He listened to Tillie's gentle flow of words, barely aware of Jana's occasional reply. His attention was riveted to the small stand of acacias beyond the garden. He rose abruptly. Damn it, there *was* someone out there.

"I'll be back in a minute," he said, cutting through Tillie's description of thrips, a miniscule insect which, if allowed a toehold, would apparently suck the juice and life from her rose bushes.

Jana put down her fork.

His brown eyes darkened, holding her in place. "There's someone moving around in the trees back there. I'm just going to check it out. Stay put," he directed before she could even rise.

She turned to the older woman. "Do you suppose it's—" One look at her aunt's harried expression stopped the words in midsentence. It was.

"I think," Tillie said decisively, "that we should join Wade before he feels compelled to do something about it." Without another word the two women hurried after him. As they drew closer he turned and waited, his hands resting lightly on his hips.

His voice was dangerously mild. "I thought I told you to wait at the table."

"You did," Jana began, "but—"

Tillie interrupted, oblivious of his scowl. "I remembered who was out here, and we came to tell you that it's all right."

Before he could say a word they were frozen in their tracks by a hoarse shout. If it was supposed to be emulating Tarzan's clarion call, Jana thought objectively, it lacked something. As a matter of fact, it sounded like a hesitant, rather unenthusiastic, "Yahooie." A tempest of leaves drew their eyes upward. Clinging desperately to a thick rope and hurtling forward at a pace that obviously exceeded his notion of a safe speed, was a stout man with protruding eyes. He wore leather boots and a safari suit. A headband held back wisps of frosted brown hair.

Wade's eyes never left the moving man. "What in holy hell is that?"

Jana choked back a giggle, covering her mouth with her hand.

Tillie's lips moved, presumably in prayer.

The man needed more than prayers. His combat boots hit the tree with a resounding smack, and he slid down the rope with all the speed, but none of the grace, of a rappeler. He landed in a pile of fragrant leaves, a tangle of limbs and rope. Heaving himself to his feet, he limped away, rope in hand, muttering. Jana didn't think he was offering up a paean of thanksgiving.

Tillie breathed a mournful sigh. "Poor Mr. Bannister. I did so hope he'd make it this time." Wade, as
he shifted his gaze to her earnest face, felt like a fighter
who had been hit once too often in the head. "He in-
herited his uncle's business," she explained, "and he's
determined to be a good manager."

He examined her face, groping to comprehend the
rationale behind her words. "Is it a logging camp?"

"Is what a logging camp?" she asked in confusion.

Rubbing the back of his neck in exasperation, Wade
felt a muscle jump in his cheek. He had no idea what
they were talking about; he wondered if Tillie did.
"His business."

"Oh, no. It's a poodle parlour. Dog grooming," she
added, at his look of blank astonishment.

"What does that have to do with..." His words
dwindled away as another voice sounded above them.
After a preliminary bout of throat-clearing, an apol-
ogetic, feminine "Hooo-haahhh" broke the silence.
Once again the rustle of leaves drew their eyes upward.

A tall, bronzed, angular woman in sneakers, cutoff
jeans, a sweatshirt and a headband drifted past, her
eyes squinted in intense concentration behind flashing bifocals.

"She'll never make it," Wade predicted, critically
eyeing her line of trajectory.

"Come on," Jana whispered encouragingly.

Tillie closed her eyes.

The three of them swayed to the left, uncon-
sciously using body English to assist the airborne
woman. For a moment it appeared to help; she bent in
the middle, thrust up with her feet and cleared the

platform. Not believing her eyes, she watched it loom before her, then begin to recede. At the last possible moment she stretched out full-length and caught her sneakered heels on the wooden planks.

The three below hardly dared to breathe, watching the stalemate. The woman hung like a kite in a windless sky, clinging to the rope, her heels caught between the slats of the platform. Her position was complicated by her glasses slipping down her nose. Jana watched as she tightened her hands on the rope and wiggled her fanny. The only visible effect was on the writhing, undulating rope. Her breath coming in shallow gasps, she lowered her head, hunched her shoulders and maneuvered her glasses up her perspiring nose. Finally, with a grunt and a heave, she kicked her feet loose, spiraled dizzily and slid to the ground. Casting a baleful look upward, she hooked the rope in the curve of her arm and trudged away.

Wade looked at Tillie. "And who," he inquired politely, "was that?"

"Mrs. Benevides." There was still a residue of pride on her face at the woman's accomplishment.

"And why is she up there?"

"So she can become an office manager."

"I'm going to hate myself for asking, but of what?"

"An acupuncture clinic in Balboa."

Wade swore in exasperation. Glaring at the two women, he touched their elbows and herded them back to the gazebo. When they were seated once again, he looked from Jana to Tillie. "Can either of you," he asked with restraint, "tell me what the hell is going on back there?" Both of them obliged. He was not visibly soothed by the combined explanation.

"—a lovely woman, a psychologist, you know."

"—a method of building confidence."

"—and poor Mr. Bannister is trying so hard."

"—have to admit that I wouldn't work that way—"

"—and Benny said it *is* successful—"

"—Mr. Franks and the others are consulting lawyers—"

"—Walter assures me that it will all work out—"

"—and they're working on a plan of action," Jana finished triumphantly.

Wade made a disgusted noise deep in his throat. "Are you telling me that a crazy woman is running an asylum behind your property and you don't plan to do anything about it because you sympathize with the inmates?"

"I don't think that's what we said at all," Tillie said indignantly. "Did we?" she said, appealing to Jana.

"No." Jana's answer was abstracted. Wade, she noted, was suffering from a common malaise, which she had tagged, for lack of a better name, the "do it" syndrome. For those so afflicted, inaction was impossible; when facing a dynamic situation, especially one wrapped in such peculiar circumstances, the instinct to *do* something—anything—was overwhelming. It simply would never occur to him, she realized, that the problem wasn't his, that he could walk away and forget it.

"You don't have to get involved in this," she reminded him. His fierce scowl should have frozen the words on her tongue; it merely reminded her of the second phase, the Don Quixote complex. Any moment now he would—metaphorically speaking, of course—mount his white charger and dash out to right the wrongs of the world.

He leaned back and regarded her with deceptive mildness. "What have *you* done about it?"

It was ridiculous to feel defensive, she told herself. After all, it wasn't as if she had known about it for days and waited for someone else to take charge. "Well, nothing," she admitted slowly. "Yet."

"Then what do you plan to do?"

She eyed him with dislike, wondering what she had ever found attractive about his deep voice. Rotten man. They shouldn't have gone after him, she decided. They should have let him wander right into the path of Mr. Bannister's combat boots. "Give me a break," she demanded. "I just found out about it this morning." She flipped through a mental card file and brightened. "Something along the lines of behavior modification probably."

Wade's snort penetrated Tillie's concentration. "Should I feed them?" she wondered aloud. "I have a wonderful recipe for carrot cake."

"No," Jana said hurriedly, remembering the barking puppy. "I'm, uh, experimenting with a new approach and I'd like to..." She couldn't think of one sensible thing that she'd like to do. Fortunately Tillie had already shifted to another aspect of the topic.

"You're not to worry, either of you," she stated, looking from Wade to Jana. "Walter assured me that this would soon end. Let's just forget about it and take all this back into the kitchen." She picked up the pitcher of iced tea and headed for the house.

Jana stacked dishes on a large tray, not breaking the reflective silence.

"When Walter decrees that all's going to end well, who usually solves the problem?" Wade asked, nudging her aside and picking up the heavy tray.

"I do," she admitted, shaking the crumbs out of the tablecloth. "And when it's all over, and I'm exhausted, Aunt Tillie shakes her head and tells me I don't trust him enough." She held open the kitchen door and pointed to a spot on the counter.

"I'd hate to have Tillie think I don't trust him, but..."

Catching a glimpse of his determined chin, Jana knew what was coming. "But?"

"I don't. I'm going next door to have a talk with Mrs. Whatsherface."

"Benjamin. Wade, why are you doing this?"

His large, warm hands cupped her face, thumbs tilting her chin until her hazel eyes met his darker ones.

"I hate seeing someone take advantage of Tillie. On the other hand, in the very near future, I have every intention of taking advantage of you. When I do, I want your full attention. And I don't want you to be exhausted."

Her eyes opened wide. She groped around and found a shred of indignation. "Is that so?"

"Definitely." His eyes gleamed as he lowered his head, touching his lips to the delicate skin at the corner of her eye.

She gave up then, at least for the moment. Folded up her indignation and tucked it in a corner. As her lashes closed she made an important discovery. His eyes weren't brown at all; there were tiny flecks of gold in them. His irises were bright, with pinpoints of golden light. Interesting, she thought, hardly daring to breathe as his lips brushed her cheek. Very...interesting.

As kisses went, it was quite chaste. At least it would have looked that way to an observer. His hands merely touched her throat and jawline; his lips brushed hers, lifted for a breathless whisper of time, then returned. That was all. Although she could feel the heat of his body, the beat of his heart, they did not touch. Then why did she feel so...chased? So anxious to be caught, to become a part of him?

Wade was breathing fast when he finally raised his head. Jana's lashes slowly lifted. His pulse jumped at the look in her eyes. A surge of recklessness joined the adrenaline pumping through his body. He touched her lips—her thoroughly kissed lips—softly with his thumb. A prudent man would get the hell out of here, he told himself. Jana's eyes darkened until they seemed all pupil, and her breath came in shallow gasps. Reminding himself that caution had never been one of his strong points, he lowered his mouth once more to hers. This time he wrapped his arms around her and drew her close.

Kissing Wade, Jana realized hazily, had its drawbacks. Hadn't she told herself that the man was hazardous to her health? Indeed she had, she assured herself. If she needed proof, the first signs of deterioration were already setting in. She was going deaf. She could no longer hear Tillie's chirpy whistle, nor the television, which Tillie had turned on full volume. All she could hear was her blood pounding, making a terrific racket in her ears. And then there was the sad case of her vision. She was blind. The light in the cheerful kitchen had faded to slate, intermittently broken by umbrellas of multicolored fireworks.

But, as with so many tragedies of life, there was compensation: her tactile sense had gone into overtime. Her hands trailed up his arms and over his broad shoulders, only to get lost in his hair. Was it possible to feel the difference in color? she wondered. To know where the lighter, sun-streaked sections merged with the other, varied shades of brown? Her shoulders and sensitive breasts rested on his chest, feeling every ripple of sinew and nerve, even the mat of prickly hair beneath his shirt. The contact deepened as he leaned back against the counter and drew her even closer.

Standing on tiptoe tightened the muscles in her legs, but they were still soft and pliant against the jean-clad hardness of his. Every nerve ending in her body reached out, testing, probing, as if exploring an alien planet. And, as the soft curve of her stomach rested in the triangular cradle of his thighs, despite the confining tightness of his jeans, she found warmth, welcome and . . . definite signs of life!

Whoa, stop, *enough*, an inner voice commanded. The man's already stated his objective—bed, yours or his—and this is pretty potent stuff. I can hear the rustle of sheets getting closer all the time. *Desist*.

Reluctantly Jana stopped her blissful rubbing of strands of his tawny hair between her fingers and dropped her hands to his broad shoulders and nudged gently. When that had no noticeable effect she put some muscle behind it. As Wade lifted his head, she noted gratefully that sight and sound returned.

"What's the matter?" he demanded. "You're not going to have the gall to pretend you didn't enjoy it?"

"Where has chivalry gone?" she wondered aloud. "Of course I enjoyed it, you idiot." Too much. Way too much. "But enough is enough. Anyway I thought you had something to do."

"I do."

"Right," she said, her memory returning, just a hair slower than her vision and hearing. "You're going to see Mrs. uh..."

"Benjamin," he reminded her with a grin.

"Right." Damn the man. She felt as if she had just run a one-minute mile, and he didn't even look ruffled, except for where her fingers had left his hair standing in tufts. And he took care of that with an unconscious gesture, running his hand through his hair, returning it to its natural wavy state.

"I don't know what good it's going to do," she continued. "Glen Franks and all the other neighbors have been to see her. The result was a big zip."

He tucked his hands in his back pockets and teetered back and forth. "You haven't seen me in action. I'm determined. And tenacious."

"Yes, I have seen you," she reminded him, thinking of his declaration in the restaurant. "And you have all the subtlety of a sledgehammer. I hope you're going to at least try to be tactful."

"Such confidence." He draped an arm around her shoulders and steered her toward the front of the house. "What do you think I'm going to do? Argue with her?"

"Probably. If she doesn't agree to stop the shenanigans by tomorrow at the latest."

Tillie was watching a Japanese science fiction movie that had a high decibel count and lots of people running first in one direction, then another. She looked up at the sound of bickering.

"Wade, dear, while you're in Mexico, will you buy me one of those pretty white shawls? Let me get you some money."

He put his hand on Tillie's shoulder, stopping her before she rose. "I'm just going next door to see your neighbor."

"Oh. Well, before you go to Mexico, be sure to let me know."

"Tillie, I haven't been across the border in several years. There isn't a thing down there that interests me."

"Then why are you going?" she asked reasonably.

"I'm not."

She shook her head tolerantly. "I don't know why you're being so secretive. There's not a thing wrong with going there. People do it all the time."

"I know they—" He broke off to scowl at Jana as she tried to muffle a giggle. "I'll be back in a few minutes."

"Want me to come along?" she asked.

"Nope." At her doubtful look, he said, "I don't know what you think is going to happen. I'm just making a friendly trip to a neighbor's house."

"Sure," she agreed. And tried to believe it.

That, of course, was before he returned with a black eye.

Chapter Six

The sound of the front door slamming lifted Jana about two inches off the plump cushion of the sofa. She caught a glimpse of Wade's shadow in the entryway as Tillie walked in from the kitchen with a raw steak in her hand.

"Time to feed your pet lion?" Jana asked, raising her brows at the messy slab of meat.

"Walter always said this was beneficial," Tillie said, with something like anticipation. "But I never had a chance to find out. How kind of Wade to—"

"Wade? *Wade?* Oh, my God." Jana bolted to the door and examined his eye with morbid fascination. The flesh around it was swollen and mottled with angry color. By this time tomorrow, she thought with a wince, he'd look like he'd lost ten rounds with a cement mixer. Stifling any further comments, she led him to the couch. It was no easy feat. He was stiff with self-contained pain and mad as hell.

He lowered himself carefully onto the center cushion and, closing his eyes, leaned back with a grunt. In midbreath, the grunt changed to a series of colorful oaths as Tillie settled the huge steak over the right side of his face. He snapped upright, clutching at it.

Jana grabbed his hand. "Leave it alone. It can't hurt. And you're going to need all the help you can get."

"What does it look like?" he asked, opening his good eye to glower at her.

"Like hell," she said briskly, knowing he neither wanted nor would appreciate her sympathy. "In ten words or less, can you tell me what you ran into?"

"Bannister's boots." He bit off his words and closed his eye, effectively shutting off any more questions.

Tillie raised scandalized brows. "You mean he *kicked* you?"

Jana had difficulty visualizing the short, rotund man even reaching Wade's eye with his fist. "Not unless he's also working on his black belt in karate," she said with a regrettable tremor.

Wade glared at her with one eye. Deciding that he had a remarkable repertoire of sinister expressions, Jana cupped her hand and gently covered his eye.

"Don't waste your energy," she advised as Tillie left the room, muttering something about Mexico. "Just lean back and relax." Moving behind the sofa, she massaged his neck and shoulders until she felt the tension ease a bit. Prodding him with a slim finger, she said, "Take a deep breath." She kneaded his muscles in silence, finally murmuring, "Another one."

Jana touched the left side of his face with gentle fingers, noting the compression of his jaw and the lines around his eye. "Try to relax the muscles around your eyes," she instructed softly. Feeling his unspoken question, she explained, "It's a shortcut. It's almost impossible for your body to be tense if those muscles are lax." Finally she felt his jaw go slack, and she smiled. He was a quick study.

Tillie tiptoed in a few minutes later. "Is he asleep?" she whispered.

The corners of Wade's mouth rose. "No, he isn't. But he's ready to remove this sloppy chunk of beef."

"Just a minute," Tillie said, heading for the kitchen. She returned with a plate, a damp wash cloth and a towel. "Here." The two women watched as he wiped his face, wincing as he patted the tender, puffy skin.

"Thanks. If I had a cup of coffee I just might decide to go on living," he say dryly, studying their absorbed expressions.

"Don't expect this kind of service all the time," Jana warned a few minutes later as she brought in a tray with cups and a steaming pot of coffee. "It's reserved strictly for wounded warriors." After he took a swallow she added, "Now, tell us what happened, and start with your eye."

Wade finished his coffee and set the cup down with a clink. "They have a tree in the yard for practice swings. I turned the corner and got clipped," he said succinctly. "That woman is impossible. She rattled on about low self-esteem and new methods and didn't hear a thing I said. She seems to think she's the modern-day savior for the depressed and downhearted. Nothing will move her except a stick of dynamite. Or maybe... Where's the telephone?"

Jana ignored the extension next to her, covered by a magazine. She pointed into the kitchen, where he would have more privacy. Deciding that scruples—at least in this situation—were expendable, she strained to follow the conversation. It was short, and all she gained from the effort was hearing him repeat the entire litany of distress to some official person. He came back with a disgruntled expression.

He sat down, resting his forearms on his knees as he leaned toward Tillie. "I called the police. They said it's your property, and you have to make the complaint."

Tillie slanted a look at the television and eyed the sci-fi film yearningly. People were still running from one side of the screen to the other in a frenzy. "I can't," she said, softly and firmly.

Jana knew that tone. Nothing could move her when she sounded like that. Nothing.

Wade didn't have the advantage of prior knowledge. He plowed on. "It's simple," he assured her. "All you have to do is pick up the phone and—" He stopped, watching Tillie's head move back and forth. "Why not?" he asked with a look that said he hoped against hope she wouldn't tell him.

"I've only been here a week or so," Tillie reminded him. "What kind of reputation would I get if I called the police and complained about every little—"

"*Little?*"

"—thing? People would think I was a bad neighbor."

"From what I've seen, the people around here might have a ticker-tape parade for you. And what kind of a neighbor is *she* being? She doesn't know the meaning of friendly relations."

"Besides," Tillie added, reluctantly turning her back on the rampant panic in the film, "what good would it do? Mr. Franks and all the others have already complained."

"They need your support. If you all stand firm—"

"Walter," she said, delivering the coup de grace, "told me I wouldn't have to do anything unpleasant. But it's nice of you to be so concerned." She pressed a button on the remote control and turned off the television. "Very nice," she added. "By the way, do you want the money for that shawl now?"

"Not now, not ever," he said firmly. "I'm not going to Mexico." He watched her until she turned into the hall. "Nice?" he asked Jana.

She smiled at his questioning tone. Obviously he didn't relate to the bland word. "Aunt Tillie said *very*," she reminded him.

"I don't feel nice. I feel grouchy, frustrated and—"

"Tense," Jana completed. "Want me to rub your neck again?"

"Yeah. But from this side." With a deft movement he leaned forward, scooped her up and deposited her in his lap. "Right there." He pointed to his nape. "Go get 'em, Tiger."

She reached around his neck and discovered what he already knew: that she needed her hands to brace herself—and they were already occupied. Her only choices were to move away or lean against him. "I take back the nice. You're not nice at all," she murmured into his shoulder. "What you are is lecherous."

"You're right," he agreed with a slow smile that she couldn't see because he was touching his lips to the soft skin behind her earlobe. She shivered and he muttered, "Ummm, that's the spot."

Jana stilled her hands and wondered fleetingly whose spot he was talking about. She worked her way under the collar of his knit shirt, then down between his shoulder blades. He slid down a couple of inches, catching her hands between his warm flesh and the cushiony back of the sofa. "I can't move," she informed him.

"I know."

"Ah. Mercy me, Rhett, whatever shall we do now?" she asked, batting her lashes. Her half smile vanished, replaced by a ripple of awareness as his teeth delicately graced her earlobe.

Wade shifted his legs, wrapped his arms around her waist and pulled her closer. A low, satisfied grunt escaped his throat as her breasts settled against his chest. "Finish what we started in the kitchen?" he suggested, lowering his head.

A blinking red light went off behind her eyelids. Danger! the overactive voice within her warned. Peril, jeopardy, hazard, *risk*! Shared showers, silken sheets, tangled limbs . . . and all that other stuff, it panted. If you don't move soon, you won't be able to, it moaned, sounding as if it were wringing its invisible hands in anxiety.

You're right, she silently agreed. The images it had conjured up, though, were most intriguing. In fact, she decided, there was something sibilantly seductive about silken sheets and shared showers...and all that other stuff. Maybe it was high time she did some in-depth research. But before she could do more than lift her head and swallow, the telephone rang. It rang a number of times, but it was Tillie's voice that finally roused her.

"Jana, Kara wants you. Pick up the phone."

It rang several more times before she could pull her hands from behind Wade, herself out of his arms and off of his lap, and grope beneath the magazine to unearth the phone. "Hi, Kara."

"It took you long enough," her cousin said on a teasing note of laughter. "Hey, you're getting almost as good as Aunt Tillie. Are you sure you didn't in-herit—"

"Don't even joke about it. She told me it was you. What do you want?" Right at the beginning she had learned that directness and blunt questions were the only methods that kept her cousin from straying into vague conversational byways. Tillie and Kara had several things in common, she had decided, once she learned her aunt's habits.

"What a thing to ask. Do I always want something when I call?"

Jana sat in a plump, roomy chair and crossed her legs. "Usually. Especially since you've been mar-ried."

"Then I'm being consistent, because I need a big favor. Please say you'll do it."

Experience had taught Jana to be wary of that par-ticular phrase. "Please say you'll do it," was saved for the big stuff. It had always been that way. Kara had been the one to dart ahead, usually straight into trouble. Jana, normally more thoughtful, trailed behind and rescued her when she was in over her head. Now, thank God, Dane Logan had assumed the task of protecting her silvery blond curls. He was the one who kept her from risking life and limb at the horse races, from being kidnapped by overeager gamblers, and found other ways to subsidize her orphanage in Tijuana. And, if the softened expression on his hard-planed face these days was any indication, he didn't consider it too onerous.

She sighed, remembering how Dane's face changed when he looked at his wife, how several of her male acquaintances regarded their particular women. Thinking of men in general brought her thoughts back to one in particular. Jana glanced up at him—and almost dropped the telephone. He was watching her the way an archeologist might have regarded King Tut's tomb: with a blaze of hunger in his dark eyes and a wealth of determination. He leaned back, stuffed his hands in the front pockets of his jeans and stretched his legs out, crossing them at the ankles. His eyes never left her. They traveled from the top of her ruffled auburn hair to her bare toes, leaving her with the shivery feeling of having been stroked by warm fingers.

Very warm, Jana thought, absently picking up a magazine and fanning herself. She noted the amusement lurking in his damnable eyes and dropped it as if it had sprouted fangs. His deep chuckle did nothing to cool her down.

"—so will you, Jana?"

"Will I what?"

Take 4 Books
-and a Mystery Gift-
FREE

**And preview exciting new Silhouette Romance novels
every month — as soon as they're published!**

Silhouette Romance®

Yes...Get 4 Silhouette Romance novel (a $7.80 value) along with your Mystery Gift FREE

SLIP AWAY FOR AWHILE... Let Silhouette Romance draw you into a love-filled world of fascinating men and women. You'll find it's easy to close the door on the cares and concerns of everyday life as you lose yourself in the timeless drama of love, played out in exotic locations the world over.

EVERY BOOK AN ORIGINAL... Every Silhouette Romance is a full-length story, never before in print, superbly written to give you more of what you want from romance. Start with 4 brand new Silhouette Romance novels—yours free with the attached coupon. Along with your Mystery Gift, it's a $7.80 gift from us to you, with no obligation to buy anything now or ever.

YOUR FAVORITE AUTHORS... Sihouette Romance novels are created by the very best authors of romantic fiction. Let your favorite authors—such as Brittany Young, Diana Palmer, Janet Dailey, Nora Roberts, and many more—take you to a whole other world.

ROMANCE-FILLED READING... Each month you'll meet lively young heroines and share in their trials and triumphs...bold, virile men you'll find as fascinating as the heroines do...and colorful supporting characters you'll feel you've known forever. They're all in Silhouette Romance novels—and now you can share every one of the wonderful reading adventures they provide.

NO OBLIGATION... Each month we'll send you 6 brand-new Silhouette Romance novels. Your books will be sent to you as soon as they are published, without obligation. If not enchanted, simply return them within 15 days and owe nothing. Or keep them, and pay just $1.95 each (a total of $11.70). And there's never an additional charge for shipping and handling.

SPECIAL EXTRAS FOR HOME SUBSCRIBERS ONLY... When you take advantage of this offer and become a home subscriber, we'll also send you the Silhouette Books Newsletter FREE with each book shipment. Every informative issue features news about upcoming titles, interviews with your favorite authors, even their favorite recipes.

So send in the postage-paid card today, and take your fantasies further than they've ever been. The trip will do you good!

Take your fantasies further than they've ever been. Get 4 Silhouette Romance novels (a $7.80 value) plus a Mystery Gift FREE!

Then preview future novels for 15 days— FREE and without obligation. Details inside.

Your happy endings begin right here.

"What do you mean what? I just told you. **Haven't** you been listening to me?"

"Of course I have," she said, refusing to admit aloud what Wade Masters already knew. "You keep fading away," she told her cousin, mentally crossing her fingers. "Run through it again."

"All right. What did you hear?"

"Nothing," Jana said, staring a hole in the floor. A long sigh blasted her ear.

"Dane and I have to leave town tomorrow. It came up suddenly, and we'll be gone for several weeks. It's come at a bad time because I've collected a lot of clothes for the kids and I told them we'd be down next weekend."

To anyone who knew Kara, the "kids" meant only one thing: the orphanage. "And?" Jana asked with foreboding.

Kara didn't bother dressing it up. "I want you to take them down for me. I know you hate the traffic," she hurried on, "but it's not always bad."

"Can't it wait until you come back?"

"Oh, Jana, you know how little they have and how little they expect. I told them we were coming, and they're all excited."

Jana remembered their bright, expectant faces from previous trips and didn't even bother with a token argument. "Why don't I come by tomorrow and pick the things up? Then, yes, I'll go next Saturday."

"You can't do that," Kara objected. "There are boxes and boxes. They won't fit in your car. You'll have to drive Dane's truck. It's all packed and ready to go."

"The *pickup*? Are you crazy? It's been years since I've driven anything with a standard shift, and I'm not about to start with that monster."

"Jana—"

"No."

"Just listen—"

"No. I'd crash into something before I went a block, and that wouldn't help anybody."

"Dane says he'll take you out for a trial run."

"I'm sorry, Kara, I'd like to help, but not that way."

Wade touched her knee. "I'll drive you."

"Who's that?" Kara asked.

"Don't be so nosy," Jana said to the telephone. "It's a huge truck," she told Wade.

"Doesn't matter. I can drive it."

"Don't you even want to know where we're going?"

"Doesn't matter," he repeated.

Jana turned back to the telephone. "You must live right. I have a volunteer chauffeur, so you can leave with a clear conscience."

"Good. He sounds interesting, but I'm too relieved to give you the third degree. I'll wait until we get back. You have a key to our place," she went on briskly. "We'll leave the truck keys in the silverware drawer. Thanks. And if your friend is as...male as he sounds, give him a big kiss for me."

Jana dropped the receiver in the cradle and turned to Wade. "My cousin is grateful and sends her thanks."

He nodded. "Where *are* we going?" he asked with idle curiosity.

Jana's smile was bland. "Mexico."

She was still smiling the following Saturday morning. Wade's expression had been a peculiar blend of disbelief and fascination, with more than a smattering of I-might-as-well-stick-around-and-see-what-else-can-happen-in-this-crazy-place.

Whatever his opinion of Tillie and her predictions, it hadn't kept him away. On the contrary. Her smile slipped a bit as she recalled the past week. Monday, wearing sunglasses to disguise a still puffy and colorful eye, he had taken her to lunch. Tuesday, dinner. Wednesday, lunch. Thursday...she winced just thinking about it.

Early Thursday evening she had opened the door to leave for an evening of darts and found Wade on the small porch, knuckles poised to knock. He was in jeans and a knit shirt and looked good enough to eat.

"What are you doing here?" she asked in surprise.

His dark eyes approved of her lavender slacks and sweater. "You mentioned the dart game yesterday. I thought I'd go with you."

"Why?" she asked, surprised. "You don't seem the type for spectator sports. Especially one this tame."

"I've never been to a pub to watch people throw darts."

Jana's voice was dry. "Don't sound so deprived. A lot of people haven't."

"I'll feed you after the game," he offered. "Win or lose."

It had been a disaster, of course. Right from the very beginning. Even before they got out of the car.

"That's it," she had told him, gesturing. "Over there."

Wade slowed down, did a double take and drove on without comment.

She nudged him. "I hate to point out the obvious, but you passed it."

He slanted a simmering glance at her. "You were actually going in there by yourself?" His tone indicated that on a scale of one to ten, she rated minus two in self-preservation.

She looked back at the dingy little place with affection. "Of course. Why?"

"You need your head examined, that's why. Look at it."

It did need paint, she admitted. And the graffiti on the front lacked distinction, but inside it was warm and friendly. She crossed her arms high on her chest and glared. "What's the matter with it?"

"It's a dump," he said flatly.

"You don't have to go in. Just turn your snooty car around and drop me off in front."

He swore, pulled an illegal U-turn and screeched into a parking place that another man was considering. The man looked as if he might object, but changed his mind after a quick glance at Wade's frozen features.

"Do you think the car will still be here when we come out?" he snarled.

"Probably not. Maybe you should take it home and tuck it in bed. I can get a ride back to my place."

The slam of his door made her jump.

He followed her inside, scowling and managing to look even larger than his normal mammoth proportions. He kept the bartender busy supplying drinks for her teammates and looked so threatening that every man who ambled over to the section of the room reserved for the dart players quickly retreated. He glared at any man who smiled in her direction or laughed too loudly. The sullen silence of the room unnerved her team, and the drinks ruined their coordination. They lost in record time, their worst defeat ever.

She stood in furious silence, tapping her feet while he opened the car door for her. "Will you tell me what that ridiculous muscle-flexing routine was all about?" she burst out as he turned the ignition key.

His gaze was frosty enough to cool even her temper. "You didn't tell me you were on an all-girl team. Or that you habitually play in dives."

"Possibly because it's none of your business." His hands were white-knuckle tight the steering wheel. She had the feeling that he'd like to wrap them around her neck. "Anyway we don't always play there. We move all around town. Sometimes the places are glitzy enough to satisfy even you."

"If I hadn't been there, anything could have happened." He gritted the words between clenched teeth. "Those guys at the bar guzzled enough beer to keep the *Queen Mary* afloat. And at one time or another every one of them tried to get over to your side of the room."

"It doesn't surprise me in the least," she replied coldly. "That's where the bathroom is."

The startled silence was finally broken by a snicker from Jana. She was visualizing the stampede that had probably taken place as soon as Wade's shoulders cleared the front door.

Wade's grin was a white flash in the dark car. He was intelligent enough, Jana noted, to remain silent.

"I'm not sure how this whole thing got started," she informed his profile as he pulled up in front of her town house, "but I don't need a bodyguard. I've managed just fine for twenty-six years without one. Almost twenty-seven," she added with scrupulous honesty. "and I don't intend to change things now."

He pocketed the keys and turned to face her, his arm resting on the back of the seat, almost touching her shoulder. "Why don't you invite me in and we'll talk about it?" he suggested soothingly.

She looked up in disbelief. "I'm neither crazy nor stupid," she assured him. What she was, was mad. And she wanted some time to walk around the house and mutter about men in general and one infuriating man in particular. Time alone, without him around to distract her or to smile the smile that had such a peculiar effect on her knees and breathing apparatus. "So let's just say good night and I'll go in. Alone."

"To sulk?" he asked with interest.

"Of course not." Just to kick a few pillows and stomp around a bit. "Why?"

Amusement glimmered in his eyes. "I just wondered if psychologists ever sulk."

"Occasionally," she admitted. "We also brood, dither and agonize. But, supposedly, we've learned nice, healthy ways to work ourselves out of those states." Belatedly recognizing his gambit for the delaying tactic it was, she opened the door and stepped outside. He caught up with her on the sidewalk.

"What time do we meet tomorrow?"

"We don't. I have a full day ahead of me. And an appointment in the evening," she added firmly as he began to protest. "Is nine okay for Saturday morning?"

He hadn't liked it, but he'd gone, giving her a whole day of relative peace and quiet in which she realized that he'd already made a place for himself in her life. She missed him. Missed his quick flashes of irritation that dissolved so unexpectedly into vivid male amusement, his eyes that darkened and lightened in concert with his moods, and, most of all, missed his arms reaching out and drawing her against his warm length.

Jana shook her head. Enough of that. She went through the house, checking doors and windows. It was almost nine; he'd be pounding on the door any minute.

Wade turned out of his driveway, driving deliberately over the attractive, winding roads. His steady pace had nothing to do with appreciation of the lush foliage or brilliant sprays of bougainvillea artistically draping stucco walls and fences. Nor was he savoring huge lungfuls of citrus-scented air. He was rigidly disciplining the inner voice that urged him to forget the speed limit and take the fastest and most direct route to the cream-colored townhouse in San Diego. It wasn't, he admitted to himself, an easy thing to do.

He glanced at the speedometer, swore softly and eased up on the gas pedal. From that first day in his office, when she had eased back in one of his chairs, gazed across his desk at him, serenely defying him not to hire her, he'd wanted her. For the company's sake, too, of course.

He stared ahead into the middle distance, turning automatically onto the freeway. It wasn't going to be easy. She was obviously not a woman to be rushed into bed, any man's bed. With characteristic patience, he'd taken her to lunch that same day in an attempt to satisfy his curiosity—and all she had wanted to talk about was business.

After that, nothing he'd done had been either characteristic or patient. He made territorial and possessive noises, and she remained politely elusive. He informed her that he would have her in his bed, and she raised her brows in disbelief. Damn it, he thought, scowling with such ferocity that the man next to him veered into the next lane, who would guess that his lady psychologist would be such a mass of contradictions? She had a smile and a laugh that could lure the birds from the trees—and a single-minded dedication to work that would send them right back. Her sweet, tempting curves were like a magnet, and her mind was full of stressors and tension relievers.

One chink he'd found in her armor was Tillie. Another—and the one that gave him what little hope he had—was the total involvement of her kisses when he managed to get her in his arms. But a couple of successful sorties, he reminded himself, did not a victory make. If he had any doubts, he only had to remember Thursday evening—and her definite withdrawal.

With a thoughtful expression he considered the trip to Mexico. Once they crossed the border and left the city traffic behind it would be a scenic drive. If he was lucky it would last long enough for him to mend some fences. If he was inventive enough he might find a convincing reason to spend the night.

He pulled up before her place and saw a curtain move in the front window. Whistling softly, he walked to the door, conjuring up visions of the two of them under a dark sky bursting with bright stars. Alone. He had never yet been alone with her for more than a couple of minutes. Privacy, he realized, was a vastly underrated commodity.

Jana opened the door. She was wearing white shorts that hugged her bottom and a white knit shirt trimmed in green. He silently reached for her key and locked the door. Yes, with a bit of luck, this trip could be a definite turning point.

Chapter Seven

You mean your cousin's psychic, too?'' Wade's question broke the long silence following Jana's carefully edited explanation of Kara's orphanage.

She nodded.

"And she supports the orphanage by picking winners at the racetrack?"

She moved her head and stopped midnod. "Not anymore. That's one thing Dane managed to stop. She attracted a rather...strange following—"

"I can imagine," Wade said dryly.

"—and Dane couldn't stand the strain. After she was kidnapped—"

"Kid—"

"—napped." Jana nodded a third time and continued. "Dane, uh, encouraged her to find other ways to raise the money."

Wade's broad smile surprised her. "I'll just bet he did." His eyes gleamed with golden points of humor as he added, "I have the feeling that I'm getting a very watered down version of this story."

"If you ever meet Kara, she can give you all the gory details. As far as that goes, I don't think *I've* ever heard the whole story." She broke off to point ahead. "There! That's it. Turn right at the wide gate."

Wade turned onto a dirt driveway that led to a large, carefully raked dirt yard with low, whitewashed buildings on three sides. He rolled to a stop and pulled the emergency brake. Before the dust had settled, youngsters were coming from all directions, tumbling out of doorways and heading for the familiar brown truck. They stopped chattering as Wade jumped down and went around to open Jana's door.

"Why the sudden silence?" he asked her. "Am I so big I scare them?"

Jana's amused expression puzzled him until he lifted her down and turned around. Straight ahead of him was a neatly trimmed beard. Tilting his chin up a couple of notches, he met steady brown eyes.

"Juanito," Jana said, moving over to give the giant a hug, "meet Wade Masters. We're standing in for Kara and Dane."

Wade measured the length and breadth of the other man with his eyes. "Little John?" he queried with a smile. "Who named you? A blind man?"

Masculine amusement lurked in both pairs of brown eyes.

"Someone with a sense of humor," Juanito replied. "Come and meet the others," he said, gesturing toward the curious children. As they approached the front porch, a pretty, plump woman with serene eyes and dark hair stepped through the doorway. "Carmella," Juanito said with obvious pride, "come meet Jana's friend."

Carmella stepped forward to hug Jana. She smiled at Wade. "Our house is yours," she said with simple formality.

Jana linked a companionable arm through Wade's. "Now the kids."

Wade was examined by twenty-two pairs of brown eyes with varying expressions. He shook hands with the older children and hunkered down to speak softly in Spanish to the little ones. He listened quietly and nodded when several boys invited him to view their dormitory. The girls insisted that he stop at their building, and within seconds a full-fledged tour was organized.

Luis, a reserved four-year-old, reached for Wade's hand and led him away. Wade's big body moved easily, towering over them all, even Ruben, the gangling teenager. It looked, Jana decided, like the Pied Piper's parade. He wasn't a bit disconcerted, she mused. But then, it would take more than twenty-two children and unfamiliar territory to throw Wade Masters off stride. He had even handled swinging bodies and a black eye with a fair amount of equanimity. Did he ever get rattled? she wondered. And if he did, would she ever be privileged to witness the event?

She watched until the last straggler rounded the corner, then turned back to Juanito and Carmella. "What's been going on down here since I last saw you?"

Juanito loosened the ropes securing the boxes in the truck and tossed them aside. He lifted two enormous cartons without apparent effort and deposited them on the long, narrow porch. "You don't want to know," he assured her.

She watched as he emptied the truck with dispatch. His English had improved in the last year, she noted. Only when he was disturbed about something did the formal intonation return.

"You know how nosy I am," she reminded him. "I want to know everything about you and the kids, and of course, the Romeros."

The Romero family consisted of five brothers, their wives, and a total of twenty-seven children. It was the brothers who had once kidnapped Kara and attempted to discover her secret of success at the racetrack. Jana's soft-hearted cousin had learned that they weren't desperados, merely unemployed construction workers trying to support their families, so she'd hired them to build new dormitories at the orphanage to replace the ones damaged by an earthquake. She also convinced her future husband and Juanito that it would be advantageous to have builders on the premises. As a result, there were five new bungalows on the far end of the ten-acre site, and twenty-seven little Romeros blended with the twenty-two orphans, only sorting themselves out when called home for meals and bedtime.

Carmella's chuckle was a warm sound. "The Romeros are a sore tip with Juanito."

"Point," Jana corrected automatically, watching Juanito disappear around the corner of the house with a large box perched on each shoulder.

"*Si*, point."

"What have they been up to?"

"Better to ask him," Carmella said, nodding in the direction of her husband as he returned for the next load. "I will be in the kitchen," she announced, ducking back through the doorway.

Jana plunked down on the next box to be carted off. "Come on, Juanito, give. What are the brothers five up to now?"

Juanito picked her up as if she weighed no more than a pound of pinto beans and eased her onto the next carton. He muttered a disgusted, *"Los Cantores Extraños,"* picked up the box she had been sitting on, and strode off.

Jana looked after him in bewilderment. The peculiar singers? Probably, she informed herself with a shake of her head, she had misunderstood.

Juanito returned, absently shifted her again, muttered, *"Los Cantores Patéticos,"* hefted the box and disappeared.

The pathetic singers? That had come across loud and clear. He'd definitely said the pathetic singers. She shifted automatically as he made his way back, retreated one more box and watched as he lifted her former seat.

He scowled at the porch rail. "They call themselves *Cantores Sin Iqualidad.*"

Singers Without Equal? Jana stared after him in disbelief. The name was appropriate, she decided numbly. She had heard them at beach parties. As entertainers they were, in a word, unique. Surely they weren't about to inflict themselves on an unsuspecting public. The closest she could come to identifying her feelings were equal parts horror and hysteria.

Perching on the porch rail, Jana waited for Juanito to claim the last box. It didn't take long.

He slung it under his arm and balanced it on his hip. "They should," he told her in a no-nonsense voice, "be called *Cuerda Pecha.*" He swiveled on his heel and thudded away.

Jana snickered. The Busted Chord. If what she had heard was representative of their talent, Juanito was a fair critic with an apt turn of phrase. She slid thoughtfully from the rail and followed an aromatic trail to the kitchen. "Carmella, tell me it isn't true!" she demanded with a grin.

Carmella looked up from peeling potatoes. Her voice was calm. "But it is."

"If I understand Juanito's grumbling," Jana said precisely, "the Romero brothers have decided to become mariachis." The world of the ubiquitous mariachi, Mexico's answer to the strolling troubadour, was in for a decided jolt, she decided.

Carmella reached for another potato. "*Sí.*"

"But you've heard them," Jana said. "They can't—"

"Sing? *Sí.*" She nodded agreeably. "They can't."

"Then why...?" She began again. "How can they possibly think—"

"They do not think," Carmella said reasonably. "They admire the *charro* costume. That is reason enough. For them."

The musicians who could afford to do so wore lavishly embroidered large-brimmed hats, short jackets and tight-fitting pants with flared bottoms. Yes, Jana reflected, the five lean men with their luxuriant mustaches and flashing smiles would look quite dazzling. Unfortunately two of them were tone deaf and none of them, at least as far as she knew, could play a musical instrument.

Carmella had a true contralto voice and often sang with Juanito as he softly strummed his guitar. She would be a fair judge of the men's talent. "How do they sound?" Jana asked.

Carmella neatly quartered a potato and dropped it in the large pan of water. She giggled softly. "They hurt the ears."

"I can't wait to hear them," Jana said with feeling, visualizing Wade's reaction. She didn't know if he was a music lover, but she had a feeling she'd soon find out.

Carmella's voice quivered. "Then you will be pleased to know that they are coming tonight to entertain us."

Jana snickered. "Do they do this often?"

"*Sí*. Too often for my poor Juanito. His ears find the sound offensive."

Jana rummaged through a drawer and found a small, sharp knife. Sitting next to Carmella, she started peeling and said, "I don't know how late we'll be staying. I'm not exactly dressed for the cool night air. I just brought a sweater with me, and I don't know if Wade even has that much."

Eyeing the growing mound of potatoes thoughtfully, Carmella murmured, "Clothes can be found for you. At least stay to eat with us."

"I'll check with Wade," Jana agreed.

The hours flew by. Jana caught up with local events as she helped Carmella in the kitchen. Once she took cold drinks outside and found Wade and Ruben bent at the waist with their heads tucked under the hood of Juanito's ancient truck. They were, she gathered, about to perform major surgery. She joined them under the hood and nudged Wade with her hip. When he didn't respond she did it again, holding out a glass of iced tea. He lifted his eyes from the fascinating mixture of greasy coils and belts, focused slowly on her curious face, took the tea and placed an abstracted kiss on the tip of her nose. She handed Ruben a glass and walked over to a cluster of girls playing jump rope.

Wade downed the drink in a couple of gulps and set the glass on the fender. His appreciative gaze followed the sway of Jana's hips, slid down to her thighs, shapely calves and ankles, and returned to her pert bottom. The sight neither diminished the heat nor soothed the ache in his loins. Muttering a soft oath, he faced the truck and gingerly settled against it.

"Where were we?" he asked Ruben. The boy returned to his list of complaints. Wade nodded, his eyes following Ruben's pointing finger in the hope that his thoughts would fall in line. They didn't. He swallowed, fighting the surge of warmth washing over his taut frame. For God's sake, he thought in disgust, he hadn't been this out of control as a teenager. Privacy, he reminded himself, that's the key. Just wangle an invitation to stay overnight and when the kids are put to bed... The kids, he thought with an inward sigh. There must have been close to fifty of them milling around. But they had to go to bed eventually. And when they did, Juanito and Carmella would no doubt want a little time together. That would leave just the two of them—himself and Jana—alone in the night, surrounded by cactus, bright stars and silence, with not one living soul to interrupt them.

He nodded his head, listening to Ruben's diagnosis. The kid seemed to know what he was doing. It was more than he could say for himself, he decided. Not that he didn't understand engines. He could probably fix one in the dark if he had to—when he could keep his mind on what he was doing. But if those bare legs and cute butt passed by even one more time, the truck would probably blow up the next time Juanito turned the key.

Dinner was an exercise in organized confusion. The children were well-behaved, but twenty-two young voices created quite a din. Everybody had a task. Some brought the food to the tables, the older children fed the babies, and others removed the dishes to the kitchen, where another crew washed them. The entire operation was quietly supervised by Juanito and Carmella.

Jana reluctantly placed her coffee mug on the table. "I suppose we should be going soon."

"Plenty of time," Wade said easily, helping himself to some more coffee.

"Why don't you stay with us tonight?" Juanito asked. "There are extra beds in the dormitories."

"Oh, I don't know," Jana began.

"Great idea," Wade said at the same time. "If we do, we can go shopping in the morning and find that shawl for Tillie. Besides, on Saturday evenings there's always a hell of a line at customs. We can leave early enough to avoid it tomorrow."

"You're sure?" Jana asked in surprise. "There's nothing you have to do tonight?"

"Not at home," he assured her.

She cast a suspicious glance at his satisfied expression before turning to Carmella. "Do you have anything I can sleep in?"

Carmella nodded. "That presents no problem. First let me see that the children have cleaned the kitchen, then I will find you something."

Juanito led them into a large room in front, where the children had already gathered, obviously a combination playroom and living room. The cement floor was covered with a brown carpet, and there were enough assorted chairs and couches to seat everyone. Carmella returned with a creamy cotton gown for Jana. She folded it and put it on a shelf, saying, "For you to use whenever you are ready."

She picked up a gleaming guitar propped carefully in the corner and handed it to Juanito. Their hands touched and lingered as he reached for it. She sat down near him with a small smile that reached her eyes. His gaze never left her as his fingers floated over the strings, picking out a soft melody. Jana sat next to Wade, her head resting on his shoulder, his hand warm on her arm. The children's voices faded as the four of them drifted in the lazy spell of soothing chords.

The mood was broken far too quickly. The murmur of distant voices grew until it sounded as if the entire population of Tijuana had converged on the front porch. Bodies poured through the door in an unbroken stream. Juanito's groan was heartfelt as he put away his guitar, and Carmella's smile became one of pure amusement.

Wade's dream of solitude and unbroken silence vanished as twenty-seven children and ten adults crowded into the room on a wave of laughter and greetings. With typical Latin courtesy Juanito introduced him to the entire crowd. Wade retained only five names, those of the men who were strutting and preening like peacocks in black, elaborately embroidered and sequined costumes.

He lifted dazed eyes to Jana. "Is this another orphanage?"

"Far from it," she assured him. "Five sets of parents and a clutch of children for each." Under cover of the confused uproar she gave him a thumbnail sketch of the Romeros.

"I don't believe it," Wade muttered. "You mean these are the same men who—"

"—kidnapped Kara," Jana agreed with a grin. "But they're harmless. Just watch for a while; you'll see."

He eyed them with fascination. "I've never seen carpenters in such fancy outfits."

"That's because they're no longer in construction. They've decided that fame and fortune await them as entertainers. They are now mariachis and call themselves the Singers Without Equal. I think we arrived in time to hear their dress rehearsal." She cut her explanation short because the brothers, amid much throat clearing and encouragement from the audience, had positioned themselves in the center of the room. With the broad-brimmed hats on, they all seemed to be the same height. And every one of them had a lean frame, luxuriant mustache and flashing smile.

The expectant hush was broken as one stepped forward. His sparkling eyes matched the brilliance of his costume, and he had a guitar draped across his chest. *"Señoras y señores,"* he began, then with a quick glance at the two Anglos in the room, he politely switched to English. "Ladies and gentlemen, I wish—" he broke off and hastily searched for the correct word "—to introduce to you the Romero Brothers!" He paused, smiling and bowing as the room exploded with applause.

"First is Trinidad!" he said, gesturing broadly.

Applause and whistles filled the room as Trinidad, with a trumpet neatly tucked beneath his arm, took a bow.

"Pepe, with his *guitarrón*!"

More applause. Pepe smiled, flashing a gold tooth, and displayed what looked like an outsize, pregnant guitar.

"Gabriel!"

Whistles and stamping feet greeted Gabriel and his violin.

"Sancho and his *vihuela*!"

More applause and hoots for Sancho and a smaller, less pregnant mandolin lookalike.

"And I," he modestly thumped the guitar on his chest, "am Domingo!"

All the brothers took another bow in the din that ensued. They followed it with a low-voiced conference that developed into a full-scale squabble.

"Is this part of the show?" Wade asked, amusement deepening his voice.

Jana noted Juanito's gloomy resignation and Carmella's mirth. "I'd like to think so," she whispered, "but I have the feeling they're just deciding what song to do first."

Domingo silenced the group by turning to the audience and adjusting the strap of his guitar. He struck a resounding chord. The sound was unlike any Jana had ever heard. He could have meant it to be C major, or possibly A minor, or any other universally accepted chord. Unfortunately, it was not. It did, however, raise the hair on Jana's arms and prepare her for what followed.

Domingo announced that the first number was a ballad of lost and lonely lovers. With that, the five burst into a lively ditty that resembled a Sousa march in a minor key. Their voices were as resounding as Domingo's strumming, and had the same hideous discords.

Wade's arm had tightened around Jana at the onslaught, and now she felt a series of tremors run down his body.

"What do you think?" she whispered.

He drew a deep breath and carefully avoided her eyes. "They're . . . enthusiastic," he stated in a controlled voice.

Jana winced as they all filled their lungs and bellowed, "Adios, adios." Goodbye. Hoping that the end was in sight, she freed her hands to lead the applause, only to fold them in her lap again as each man drew another great breath.

"And tenacious," Wade muttered.

The lovers apparently were having a rough time of it, because the song seemed to have no ending. Occasionally one man would take a break while the other four nobly carried on.

"And have amazing stamina," Wade said, still not looking at her.

Abruptly, as if someone had crimped their vocal chords, the men stopped singing.

"What happened?" Wade asked, stunned by the sudden silence.

"Clap," Jana muttered. "I think it's over."

Juanito jumped to his feet. "Thank you, my friends; it was a pleasure to hear you sing your new song. We must do this again sometime." He hastily shook hands with all five men. "Some other evening we must hear another song. Isn't that so, Carmella?"

"Indeed," she murmured. "I can hardly wait."

There was a hurried conference among the five brothers. Domingo turned with a beautiful smile. "Amigos, just for you we have another song." The men tussled with straps and strings to produce their instruments.

Juanito dropped down on the couch with a stricken look.

Wade, who was getting to his feet, fell back with a muffled groan.

Domingo threw back his head and began to sing, strumming discords madly to keep up with the lively tempo. Pepe, gold tooth flashing, leaped in with his *guitarón*, while Sancho stroked his *vihuela* with a pick. The three stringed instruments, sounding as though they had never been tuned, were joined by a fourth as Gabriel sawed the violin. Trinidad puffed his cheeks and blew into the trumpet, occasionally producing a thin bleat.

The song had to do with another lover who suffered untold miseries when his lady left him to follow a matador. Each new verse was a variation on the theme of his wretchedness. The four men, each flailing his instrument and inspired by Trinidad's trumpeting, sang lustily of torment, woe, anguish, agony and infelicity. They ended on a triumphant note of clashing chords and turned expectant faces to their adult audience.

Juanito was speechless.

Carmella was overcome.

Wade slowly rose to his feet.

Jana watched him anxiously.

"That was without a doubt," Wade said deliberately, "the most—"

"Innovative musical program we've ever heard," Jana finished with a rush.

Domingo, Pepe, Gabriel, Sancho and Trinidad beamed and shuffled their feet. They conferred briefly, and Domingo said, "For friends such as you, we have one more little song—"

Juanito jumped to his feet. "No! It is too much! Not another one."

Carmella rose and slid her hand into the crook of his arm. Smiling at the five men, she said, "What Juanito means is that we must savor what you have shared with us tonight. Any more would surely detract from your gift."

The brothers removed their outsize hats, held them over their hearts and bowed. One more round of applause broke up the party. The Romero mothers collected their children and herded them out the door. Carmella called her girls and promised to meet them at the dormitory. Juanito rose to round up the boys.

Domingo secured his guitar and plucked at Juanito's shirt sleeve. "We will be here when you come back," he promised. "We want to discuss business with you." He thumped his guitar in excitement and announced, "Next week we will sing at the cantina and we want you to be our arranger." There was a buzz of whispers behind him, and another hurried conference. He listened, nodded and turned back to Juanito. "Our manager. That is what I mean. We want you to make the business arrangements."

Juanito's appalled glance took in Carmella's expressionless face and the shaking shoulders of his two friends. "We will talk when I return," he promised grimly. "Believe me, we will talk." He swung on his heel and left the room.

Carmella touched Jana's shoulder and murmured, "There are jackets in the closet if you wish to go outside. I will be back later, when the girls are settled."

Wade watched her leave and glanced over his shoulder at the musicians. He dropped his hand to the small of Jana's back and gently nudged her toward the closet. "Let's get out of here. I don't like the way they're fingering those instruments."

He grabbed a poncho and one of Juanito's jackets. Opening the door, he hustled Jana outside.

"What's the hurry?" she protested.

His chin was set at a determined angle. "I don't want to listen to another saga of lonely lovers," he stated unequivocally. Dropping the poncho over her head and shrugging into the jacket, he added, "I just want to be alone with you for a while. Is that asking too much?"

Chapter Eight

Too much? Jana wondered, buttoning the neck of the colorful poncho. Hardly. Especially considering that she wanted the same thing.

"Nope," she said, linking her arm through his. "Where are we going?"

He pointed out through the wide gateway. "What about the road? There's not much traffic. We'll have it pretty much to ourselves."

"Good," she said, turning with him. "I'm not too wild about following some of these paths in the dark."

They stopped at the edge of the paved road, and she pointed to the illuminated sky to their left. "Look at the lights of the city. It's hard to believe that we're just a few miles from the bustle of Tijuana."

He nodded, turning so the lights were behind them. "It's pretty cool out here. Are you warm enough?"

"Um-hmmm." The sound was a soft sigh of contentment.

Wade stopped to examine the voluminous folds of the poncho, which fell to Jana's thighs. He lifted the edge closest to him, slid his arm inside, settled it around her waist and urged her forward again. "Do you have one of these things at home?"

Jana cleared her throat. His hand spanned her ribcage, his thumb resting just below her breast. "No."

His eyes gleamed at the slightly breathless tone. "Damn good idea. If the word gets out to enough men, it could put the coat industry out of business."

Jana's gaze locked on his face as his words filtered through her somnambulant state. A surge of exasperation drew her brows together. She had sounded like a lovesick idiot. It was no wonder she couldn't keep him at arm's length. But at the moment, with his large hand leaving a warm imprint, she was having a hard time recalling why she even wanted to.

The clinic, she reminded herself with a mental shake. Remember the master plan? Two years and you'll be there; you'll have accomplished what you set out to do. You'll be a partner in a thriving business and won't have to spend so much time working.

I don't know, she wondered doubtfully. The clinic is doing pretty well. Why can't I take what he's offering?

Because "pretty well" isn't *there*, commented her sterner self. And just what *is* he offering? A sexy body in a king-size bed? For how long? A couple of nights? A week? A month or two? Come on, Jana, you can do better than that. Feeling that sexy body glued to her side, she had her doubts.

Jana!

All right, all right!

She cleared her throat to get his attention and groped for her business voice. "You know something? We never did set up those preliminary appointments."

He stopped as if he had run into a brick wall and glared down at her.

She had his full attention, she realized.

His other hand found its way beneath the poncho. "You know something?" he half-snarled.

She shook her head.

"I don't give a damn." His hands slipped down the hollow of her waist and back to cup the sweet swell of her buttocks. Easing her against his hard frame, he said, "Why do you think I grabbed these jackets and got us out of the house so fast?" He punctuated his question with a soft kiss at the side of her mouth.

"Claustrophobia?" she wondered aloud, her arms settling on his shoulders.

Amusement curled his lips, but they still managed to investigate the othe   le of her mouth. "No. And you better believe it wasn't to talk business."

"I give," she whispered, her hands delicately kneading the back of his neck.

"I wish you meant that," he muttered, wrapping his arms around her, one hand on her nape, the other slipping under the elastic band of her shorts, once again cupping the tantalizing curve.

Flesh against flesh, Jana thought dreamily, feeling the warmth radiating from his hand. That same hand was urging her closer, fitting her to him like a second skin, showing her the measure of his need, his desire.

She nestled closer still, sliding her arms around his neck, stretching to touch his lips.

A half sigh, half groan sounded deep in Wade's throat. This woman was going to drive him crazy. The sudden realization, during the last week, that her wide hazel eyes were unmarked by experience had been electrifying. The knowledge had released desires he didn't even know he possessed. He had never, for God's sake, fantasized about capturing a virgin, dragging her off to some secluded place and initiating her in the rites of love. Until now.

Never had he been so preoccupied with the memories of a woman's swaying hips that he couldn't work. Until now. He had never known that an involuntary gasp of surprise following a woman's first surge of pure passion could be so exciting. Until now. Never had he been so lacerated by his own needs and the knowledge that he would die before he harmed one auburn hair of a particular woman's head. Until now. He lowered his head, meeting her warm lips with his own.

Jana's sigh was a sound of pure pleasure. A couple of her senses had done their disappearing act again. Her world was dark and silent. But she could feel, and she decided that being plastered to Wade from her lips to her toes was like embracing a furnace. Two years of deprivation was an awful long time, she reflected. After all, she hadn't experienced *this* when she formed her master plan. Maybe eighteen months would do it. Or a year. Six months if she worked like the very devil.

The need for air hit them both at the same time. Jana rested her head on Wade's chest, listening to the accelerated drumming of his heart. It matched the double-time beat of her own. Her lips curved in a small smile that any woman in the world would have recognized.

Lifting her head, she asked "Why?"

Wade looked down in surprise. "Why what?"

"I don't know. You asked me something and I was supposed to figure out why."

"Oh."

She propped her elbows on his broad chest, chin in hands, and watched him.

A reluctant grin curved his lips. "Damned if I know," he admitted.

She nudged him with her elbows. "Come on. This could be important."

Her hazel eyes were alight with expectation. He suppressed the urge to toss her over his shoulder and disappear into the night. How was a man supposed to think when he was being scrutinized like that? he wondered. When all he really wanted was to keep this elusive creature in his arms, to run his hands over her soft curves, to be left alone long enough to . . .

His hands tightened fractionally around her waist as he remembered. "I asked you why you thought I rushed you out of the house."

"Oh, that's right."

Amusement caused him to momentarily ease his taut stance as he watched her expressive face. She concentrated as if she were working out a complicated mathematical equation, he thought. Suddenly she relaxed, dropping her head back on his chest, her body seeming to flow around his. Just as quickly, tension racked his frame.

Her cheek nestled in the hollow of his shoulder. "I give," she said with a contented sigh.

An amused rumble vibrated in Wade's chest. "You did that a few minutes ago, and look where it led us."

She rubbed her cheek against the soft fabric of his knit shirt. "Is that a complaint?"

"Hardly." His hands slipped down to the small of her back and gently pressed her flat stomach to his aching loins. Then, with a sharp sigh, he switched his grip to her hips and moved her away. Turning her around to face the orphanage, he adjusted his long stride to her shorter one.

Unrestricted by the swinging folds of fabric, he wrapped his arm around her waist as they walked. "I really do like this thing," he said, fingering the button at her neck. "What's it called?"

"A poncho."

"Nice."

"It doesn't do much for the figure," she commented as he steered her back through the gates.

"It, uh, has other advantages," he said, and demonstrated one by tracing her spine from beginning to end with his thumb. To emphasize the point, he left his hand cupping what he found at the end.

"I see what you mean," she said, increasing her pace.

He led her to a bench on the edge of an oval cactus garden. The end nearest them was framed by large agaves, similar to the century plant, with thick fleshy leaves tipped by long, sharp needles.

"It looks like Carmella is still with the girls," he commented. "The lights are still on in the dorm. And

I'm not going back in until those madmen have gone home."

Jana giggled. "Juanito may need rescuing."

"Tough. As far as I'm concerned, it's every man for himself." He sat down and tugged at her hand, drawing her onto his lap.

Jana gingerly eased down on his thighs, raising mental brows at her uncharacteristic docility. What the hell, she thought, with a hunger that surprised her. If it's going to be business as usual tomorrow, I can at least enjoy tonight.

Wade gathered her to him and leaned back on the high-backed wooden bench. Resting his chin on a coil of auburn hair, he said, "Listen."

Jana stilled. "To what?"

"Crickets. There's not another sound."

Wiggling until she found a comfortable spot, she said, "I guess you're used to it."

"What do you mean?" Wade sounded oddly vague.

"Rancho Santa Fe isn't exactly noisy at night."

"You're right. And I like it that way."

"Lucky man," she said lazily.

He tucked a strand of hair behind her ear. "Why?"

"San Diego's a great place to live, but there's hardly ever the kind of quiet we're talking about. Even in the middle of the night you can hear the cars on the freeway, or just street noises."

He nodded in lazy agreement. "I have to work in it during the day, but this is what I like at night: crickets, whispers of night sounds and moving shadows." He just had time to realize that there was no breeze and wonder why shadows were moving when the night seemed to explode around their bench.

"Adios, adios!" five voices thundered in the silence. Five men sauntered out from behind the agaves, protecting five outsize hats from the thorned fronds. Once they were clear of the cacti, they clapped the sombreros on their heads and groped with the straps confining their stringed instruments.

Trinidad, having tucked his trumpet in the tall crown of his hat, had the advantage. He filled his lungs and blew three separate and distinct notes. While the others boomed, "Adios, adios," and wrestled their instruments into position, he stopped and looked at the shiny horn. He was clearly astonished at what he had just accomplished.

The song they raced through was one Wade and Jana had not heard. The lovers had either been reunited, or it was a different pair. They were eloping with their parents' consent and saying goodbye to their parents, their god-parents, their aunts and uncles, nieces and nephews, family friends, the horses, dogs, cats and burros.

"Adios!" Domingo had won the race. He threw back his head and yipped in celebration as his fingers moved with uncaring abandon over the strings. Speed and volume were obviously his top priorities.

Pepe was a close second with his gourdlike *guitarón*. "Adios!" he bawled, strumming a jangled discord.

Trinidad, buoyed by his recent success, called out an absent "Adios," licked his lips and raised his trumpet. He sounded two notes, neither of which had any relation to the song, before they dwindled away to a breathy sigh.

Gabriel wiped perspiration from his forehead, tucked the violin beneath his chin and raised the bow. He sawed the strings the same instant that Sancho strummed his *vihuela*. The combined sounds were awesome.

For the first time since Jana had met him, Wade was speechless.

After the first convulsive shock had ripped through the two of them, pulling them upright, they sat in stunned silence. Jana lifted her head from his stiff shoulder, glanced at his set features and thought longingly of her camera. His affronted glare was worth preserving.

Wade opened his lips, looked down to her eyes, which were brimming with laughter, and closed them again. He slumped back against the bench, taking Jana with him. Tremors ran through her body into his, and she muffled peculiar, little moaning sounds against his shoulder.

A reluctant grin creased his face. This wasn't exactly the way he'd planned for the evening to end, he conceded, wincing at a particularly off key "Adios." He had hoped to have her tremble in his arms, but with passion, not mirth. His hands drifted over her body as it rested so confidently against his. Lines of determination replaced his smile. Tomorrow was another day, he reminded himself. There was always tomorrow.

The sight of Wade's smile wound the five men up for a spectacular finish. With a great clashing of chords and one last piercing note from Trinidad's trumpet, they sighed one final "Adios," removed their hats and bent forward in a series of flamboyant bows.

Jana was forever grateful that she had turned around in time to witness the end of the song.

Pepe, the last to take a bow, backed into a two-inch needle of the agave. His agile leap sent him careening against Trinidad, whose trumpet flew into the air. He bounded to catch it and jostled Domingo, whose guitar smacked Sancho on the rear. Sancho staggered into Gabriel, who maintained his balance by impaling his violin bow in the ground. Baleful scowls were exchanged; then one last smile was flashed at their audience as they shuffled back into a ragged line.

Jana jumped to her feet, offered strangled compliments and bolted for the house.

It was early afternoon before they crossed the border. Jana had visited with Juanito and Carmella for an hour or so before making her way to the girls' dormitory and slipping into one of the narrow beds. Wade had not returned to the house.

She awoke to the sounds of laughter and hissing noises as the older girls tried to quiet the little ones. Her mattress jiggled, and she opened one eye. Carmen, a charmer of eighteen months, crawled up from the foot of the bed and snuggled next to Jana, sharing her pillow. Nose to nose, they stared at each other.

Drawing the baby close and giving her a quick hug, Jana's heart did a flip. All these little brown-eyed girls reminded her of Wade. What would it be like to carry his baby? she wondered. To feel life fluttering and watch the daily changes in her own body?

Giving Carmen a quick kiss, she kicked off the sheet and single blanket as she counseled herself. Forget it. What you've got here is a classic case of apples and oranges. You're talking love, commitment and marriage; so far, he's mentioned bed and sex. Giving a mental shrug, she swung Carmen up and turned to face the other girls.

"Come on, kids. Let's surprise Carmella. We'll get dressed and tidy up the place so we'll be ready for breakfast."

Keeping busy helped. She didn't think of Wade until she faced him over the breakfast table. Although his hair was still damp from the shower and he was freshly shaven, he didn't look very rested, she decided. He raised his coffee cup in greeting and smothered a yawn.

She helped Carmella and the older girls wash the dishes while Wade and Ruben had one last conference under the hood of Juanito's truck. Wade came in to wash off the grease just as they put away the last few plates.

He dried his hands and wiped away the splash marks on the sink. "If we're going to find Tillie's shawl, we'd better get going."

She nodded.

You'd think we were leaving for the moon, she reflected five minutes later. Wade opened the truck door for her. The children milled around Carmella and Juanito, and called out in a mixture of Spanish and English.

"Be careful. Watch for crazy drivers."

"Thanks for the clothes."

"Goodbye."

"Come back soon."

"Thanks for helping with the truck," Ruben said.

Wade slammed her door and moved to his side. Climbing in, he said, "Let's go. I see the Romero clan coming, and I'm not up to them this morning."

Waving goodbye, he reversed the truck and eased out of the yard to the main road. With a final wave they were on their way. Fifteen minutes later they were threading their way through the heavy traffic of Tijuana and maneuvering into a parking place.

Before Jana could clamber down, Wade lifted her, his hands lingering at her waist.

She pointed, doing her level best to deny the breath backed up in her lungs. "I think there's a place across the street."

"Wait a minute." He grabbed her wrist as she started to jaywalk. Leading her to the corner and a traffic light, he said, "We need every advantage we can get here. I think every taxi driver in the place has a death wish."

It took no time at all to find a shawl for Tillie. What held them up was Wade's search for a poncho. Jana lost count of the ones she modeled.

Wade finally nodded in satisfaction. "That's it."

"It" was a black wool circle of material that fell to midthigh. It had a four-inch fringe and two escape hatches. She could get in and out of it by simply dropping it over her head or by undoing the large black buttons down one side.

Jana ran her fingers over the soft fabric as Wade dickered for it. Nothing was done simply south of the border, she reflected for the hundredth time. You never just pulled out money and paid for something.

She had learned that some years before, the first time she asked the price of a gleaming leather purse.

She had handed it back when the vendor told her one hundred dollars. A bargain, he assured her. Undoubtedly it was, she answered, and said that in all honesty she didn't have that much to spend. And that, she had assumed, turning away, was that.

"Ninety," he had called after her.

She had turned back, her brows rising in genuine surprise. She had never in her life haggled over a price.

"Eighty," he said, scowling ferociously.

She shook her head regretfully. Eighty wasn't bad, but she still didn't have it.

"Seventy."

"You're kidding," she said in disbelief. It was a steal at that price.

"Sixty," he said between clenched teeth.

She eyed him in amazement, laughing at the ridiculous situation. "I don't believe what you're saying."

"Fifty," he snarled, "and that's my last offer."

She would have sold her grandmother, if she'd had one, to take advantage of that bargain. Fortunately she wasn't driven to that extreme. She had fifty dollars and some change on her. "I'll take it." She had given him the money and walked away with a purse that was still her pride and joy.

Now, watching Wade and the shopkeeper enjoying themselves at the top of their lungs, she waited patiently, knowing the outcome would be equitable and satisfying to both parties. After a few more minutes Wade reached for his wallet.

"Thank you," she said rather formally as they approached the truck. "I'm going to enjoy wearing this."

He nodded, muttering something that sounded like "me too" as he slammed her door and walked around to his.

There was no line at customs, and within minutes they were back on their own side of the border.

After mentally practicing several approaches, Jana opted for the direct one. "I waited for over an hour last night. Juanito and Carmella were finally yawning in my face. What happened to you?"

His slanted glance was loaded with sheer, masculine appraisal. "I knew I wasn't going to get any sleep, so I went off with the Romeros."

Her gurgle of amusement curled around him, weaving a web of warmth and contentment.

Her eyes were wide with blatant curiosity. "What did you do?"

He grinned. "I taught them some more songs."

"You did *what?* What kind of songs?" she asked with foreboding.

The creases in his cheeks deepened. He kept his eyes on the road as he sang softly.

"That's enough!" she cried a few minutes later, wiping her eyes. She was grateful she had no mascara on. "Those are really awful," she said in awe. "Where'd you learn stuff like that?"

"You pick up all kinds of useful information in college," he informed her.

They locked the pickup in Dane's garage, retrieved Wade's car and headed for home. Wade's home.

"How about a swim and some lunch? Then I'll take you back to Tillie's."

Why not? she wondered defiantly, daring that other voice to protest. Today's Sunday. A day of rest, a day of recreation. Monday's time enough to get back to work and...make some decisions. Decisions about this man, her job, his pursuit, her reactions. She didn't ask herself why they required such consideration, or why she faced them with such uncharacteristic reluctance.

"Sounds good," she said, deliberately shrugging away her gloomy thoughts and smiling up at him. "I don't have anything to swim in, though."

"My sister always keeps some stuff here. You're just about her size."

Jana blinked. "You have a sister?"

He pulled up in his driveway. "Did you think I'd been hatched? I have a sister, a brother and two parents." He looked down at her. "Is that so unusual?"

"No. Of course not." Somehow she'd never gotten around to picturing him with a normal family. You just didn't expect marauding pirates, *elegant*, marauding pirates to come equipped with relatives, she told herself.

He unlocked the front door and ushered her inside the house. "Let me show you where Sue's things are." Opening a closet, he waved a hand. "Help yourself. Meet you at the pool."

Jana sorted quickly through the clothes and found a fairly conservative jade bikini that fit reasonably well. Over it she wore a thigh-length white terry cover styled like a man's shirt. She looked in the mirror and frowned. More decisions. Button all the buttons and look like a contemporary of Aunt Tillie's, or leave them open and be a walking invitation? Impatiently she touched the third button from the top and began fastening. When she reached the bottom she checked the mirror again. There is no right or wrong to this, she reminded herself. It's strictly a matter of preference. Well, in that case, she decided with a slow smile, undoing the fourth button won't hurt.

When Jana walked into the kitchen she found Wade at the sink surrounded by leaves of lettuce, tomato slices, avocado, chicken, mayonnaise, butter and several varieties of bread. Sweating cans of drinks stood nearby.

She slid onto a stool and propped her chin in her hand. "You don't mess around, do you?"

"I've done all I plan to do," he assured her. "The rest is cafeteria style." He held out a hand to her. "Come on, dig in."

He'd even had time to put on his suit, she noted. As if she could help noticing, she thought dryly. It was brief. Very. And honey-brown, the same color as his body. It was like standing next to a nude giant, she thought distractedly, debating the merits of rye over wheat or sourdough. Grabbing blindly for bread— who cares what kind? she thought wildly—she threw together a sandwich, dropped it on a plate, grabbed a drink and headed for the patio.

Girl, she informed herself sternly, dropping down on a lounge chair, you have got to pull yourself together. Wade came out with his hands full and used his bare foot to scoot an aluminum chaise next to hers. Stepping over the end of the chair, he lowered himself and stretched out beside her.

He polished off his enormous sandwich before she had even made a dent in hers.

"Are you going to eat that whole thing?" he inquired, covetously eyeing the half still on her plate.

She slapped at his hand. "Yes. If you want more, go make another one."

He leaned back with a grin and watched her eat. Jana averted her eyes. She couldn't keep an eye on him and swallow at the same time, she found. She ate every crumb, wiped her mouth on the napkin and reached out to put her plate on a round, tiled table.

"Are you going to stay wrapped up in that thing all day?" Wade asked, pointing to the terry shirt.

"This? I forgot about it," she said. His expression informed her that he didn't believe it for a minute.

Jana sat up, unfastened the remaining buttons and shrugged out of it. She turned just in time to see Wade reaching for her. He plucked her out of her chair and settled her next to him.

Clutching his shoulder so she wouldn't tumble off, she pointed out the obvious. "There's not room for both of us."

"Sure there is. All we have to do is—"

Jana jumped as a cordless phone next to the chair shrilled. Wade muttered something she was just as glad she didn't hear.

"Five will get you ten that it's Aunt Tillie," Jana said with a grin.

"Can't be," he said complacently. "I've got an unlisted number and she doesn't know it."

"That's never stopped her before," she informed him as it rang again.

"Why would she call here?" he asked, puzzled.

Jana's eyes drifted down over their bodies, seemingly bonded together. "She has this incredible sensitivity," she began.

"My God," he said in horror. "You mean she can see us?"

Jana blinked. "I don't know. I've never really thought about it."

"I don't believe it," he mumbled, wincing at another shrill ring.

"Don't worry," Jana said, biting back a smile. "She's discreet. She always has a valid reason for calling."

Wade dropped her back on her own chair and scowled. "You're wrong," he stated definitely, reaching for the phone. "It won't be her."

He lifted the phone to his ear. "Hello," he half-snarled.

"Wade, dear," Tillie's clear voice lifted the hair on his arms. "I just wanted to thank you for the lovely shawl."

"You haven't even seen it," he said, shaken.

"I haven't?" she asked in surprise. "But I know it's lovely. Walter even said so. And I do want to thank you."

Chapter Nine

"You're late," Ken announced blandly as Jana rushed through the door on Friday afternoon.

She tossed a harried glance at the large, round clock on the wall. "Just fifteen seconds," she said, looking around hopefully for support. What she saw were three identical grins. "All right," she grumbled, digging in her purse. "All I can say is, this is going to be one hell of a Christmas party."

"Whose fault was it this time?" Ken asked as she dropped a one dollar bill in the cookie jar.

Jana sat down with a scowl. "The United States Weather Bureau."

"Original," Laura conceded.

"Reaching a bit, I think," Tish decided.

"I'll bite," Ken said amiably. "Why?"

"If they hadn't decided that San Diego has the only perfect climate in the United States, then publicized the fact, we wouldn't now be the seventh largest city in the country and have new skyscrapers popping up every day, with streets tied up with construction and traffic backed up to God only knows where,'' Jana said heatedly, without once having to come up for air.

"You were lucky to make it this early, if you were in that mess downtown,'' Tish said with feeling.

"Does that mean I get my dollar back?''

"No!'' three voices said at the same time.

Jana shrugged. "Just asking.''

"Are we ever going to get down to business?'' Ken asked in a failing voice. "I have an appointment later this afternoon.''

Ken and Tish were just beginning an assignment with one of the new biomedical research and development companies in town; Laura was in her second week at an aerospace company's corporate headquarters. Everything was under control.

"And I,'' Jana commented, "plan to be at Wade's place full-time beginning Monday.''

"How's it going?'' Ken inquired. "Any problems?''

"With Wade or the job?'' she asked dryly.

He grinned. "Whatever.''

"Anything kinky?'' Tish assumed a hopeful expression. "Ken was a total flop in that department.''

"Ken, if you don't take her in hand, I'm going to buy her one of those Victorian erotica books and turn her loose,'' Jana threatened.

He leaned forward and tugged gently at one of Tish's soft brown curls. "I've been thinking of doing just that.''

"Victorian porn?'' Tish asked, still hopeful.

"Taking you in hand."

"Dull," she said distinctly. "Very dull."

He looked directly at her and smiled slowly. "Not the way I'll do it," he promised.

Jana looked from Tish's stunned expression to Ken's bland one. Her brows shot up in tandem with Laura's.

Clearing her throat in the thoughtful silence, Jana said, "Since the work situation is well in hand, may I have your opinions on something else? It's about Aunt Tillie."

Within seconds she had a rapt audience. When she finished, despite her heroically neutral tone, Ken's eyes were popping. "Bodies?" he asked in a quivering voice. "Swinging?"

"From trees?" Tish's voice had a tinge of awe.

Laura giggled.

Tish covered her mouth with her hand and blinked watery eyes.

Ken's shoulders shook. He guffawed. "Boots in his *eye*?" He pounded the arms of his chair. *Acupuncture* clinic?"

After the din died down, Laura passed out tissue and they all wiped their eyes.

"What can we do to help?" she asked.

"Can I come and watch?" Ken wanted to know.

Jana ignored him and answered Laura. "I opened my big mouth and told Wade I'd figure out a way to discourage them. I want your suggestions."

Ken jumped up. "I've got it."

Three pairs of eyes turned on him.

"I just joined a rifle club. We could put in blank ammo and use them for target practice."

"Very funny," Jana said with restraint. "I was hoping to use behavior mod, not dent them."

"You could chop down the trees," Tish suggested.

Jana shook her head. "They're all on that woman's property. I'd probably end up in jail."

"You could slip over at night and cut the ropes—no, that wouldn't work," Laura decided. "They'd just replace them, and you'd still have the problem."

"Will you listen to us?" Tish demanded. "Four psychologists and between us we can't think of one legal way to handle this."

"Pathetic, isn't it?" Jana agreed. She looked around at three blank faces and sighed. "Well, if you think of anything, let me know."

"What are you going to be doing in the meantime?" Laura asked.

"I'm spending the weekend with Aunt Tillie. With any luck at all, I'll come up with something."

Luck was not exactly perched on her shoulder shouting in her ear, Jana decided six hours later. She lay back on a lounge chair in the gazebo looking out toward the acacias. The air was still warm and it was several hours before dusk. According to Aunt Tillie, the witching hour was almost upon them. The tree people would soon be in action, the volume of their shouts increasing with every swing. They were amazingly law-abiding, though. She had to give them that. They never once crossed over the property lines. Too bad the noise couldn't be confined to their side. Instead it radiated out, startling the neighbors, ruining their digestion and their dispositions. Poor Glen Franks couldn't even hit his practice golf balls anymore. He looked with loathing at the trees and complained that when your concentration was blown, so was your coordination.

Coordination? Jana slowly rose to a sitting position, not even breathing. An idea like this came once in a lifetime, she decided, and she wanted to let it blossom, not kill it at birth. Could it be that simple? It could. Of course it could! She leaped down the steps and ran for the house.

It took her a while to find it. Aunt Tillie kept moving it around the house. She tracked it down in the dining room and patted it fondly on its backside. "Gong, you and I have things to do," she murmured.

It shivered an answer.

Jana peeked into the living room. Aunt Tillie was engrossed in another Japanese science fiction movie. Once again a panicked crowd skittered to the left, spotted the monster and did an about-face, screaming with every step. There was, of course, something equally awful on the right. Jana was grateful that she couldn't see what it was. Where does she find these things? she wondered. Wherever it came from, she was grateful that it was keeping her aunt occupied. And, with the decibel level so ear shattering, Tillie certainly wouldn't hear any noise from outside.

Rolling the gong through the house was a piece of cake. Even maneuvering it down the back stairs and along the garden path wasn't so bad, Jana decided. Where it got sticky was behind the gazebo. The grass was neither well-cultivated nor manicured. It had either returned to Mother Nature or never been relinquished. The ground was a mass of weeds, bushes and prickly shrubs. There was no straight pathway for a wheeled vehicle six inches wide, a yard long and a yard high. Jana pushed, pulled and cussed.

Panting, she settled behind the droopy boughs of an acacia and kicked a few tufts of weeds aside to level the ground. The gong settled in place with a shimmering sigh.

Now all she had to do was wait for the first victim.

He, or rather they, came sooner than she had expected. First came the call. She tilted her head and listened critically. Not bad, she thought. Rather like a yodeler who swallowed a fly, but not bad. At the same time that she spied a tall, bony man with freckled arms breaking through the trees, she spotted Wade batting aside bushes and making his way toward her. She waved at him and turned her attention back to the trees.

Freckles was clutching the rope between his gangly legs, and he was far too close to the ground. Too close for his purpose, she thought grimly, but not for mine. He swooped to the lowest point of his flight just as Wade stepped through the last barrier of brambles. As Jana swung the padded stick with a straight arm, Wade poked his head through the bushes.

He saw Jana swing, saw the stick hit the gong dead center. Before he could even blink the small bower was reverberating with dazzling, earsplitting sounds, a brassy cacophony that seemed to splinter notes and toss the shards into the air. His outraged glare turned to Jana, then followed her fascinated gaze to a sight he would never forget.

At the sound of the gong, the tall man's hands loosened on the rope for a fateful second. He slid down, hitting the ground at a run and not stopping until his hands clutched the knot at the end of the rope. At that point his feet flew out from under him and he dropped down in a sitting position on the hard, dry dirt. He looked around in bewilderment. Slowly, hand over hand, he pulled himself up until he was on his feet. He turned a full circle, still hanging onto the rope, examining every clump of bushes with suspicion.

Jana dropped down, sitting on her heels, and motioned for Wade to join her. He knelt beside her. Before he could say a word she put her hand to his mouth. "Shhh," she murmured. "Wait until he goes."

With one last glare, the tall man swatted dust from his pants, grabbed the end of the rope and headed back to his starting place.

Jana turned eyes gleaming with success to Wade. "What do you think?" she whispered.

"I think I've got a headache," he said grimly.

Jana turned to watch Freckles disappear. Her voice was absent. "Probably tension."

Wade stiffened. "I told you before, I'm not bothered by stress."

Jana watched him rub the back of his neck. "Tension," she confirmed calmly.

Wade exploded in a whisper. "It doesn't surprise me at all. Do you realize that before I met you, my life was quite ordinary? I never went out with a woman who pranced around in dingy bars. I never knew one who had at least five certified lunatics for friends. And I never dated one with an aunt who lived next to a nuthouse and could see down telephone wires."

Jana patted his knee. "Must have been dull," she commiserated.

His lips twitched in a reluctant grin. "Damnably," he agreed. He dropped his hand over hers, pinning it to his knee.

An agitated dipping and swaying of bushes and acacia boughs, accompanied by a few muttered grunts, brought them to their feet. For one moment of sheer panic Jana remembered a documentary she had recently watched about a wild boar charging through the brush in the wilds of Australia. There aren't any here, she reassured herself. Not in Rancho Santa Fe.

The heavy-breathing frame of Glen Franks eventually broke through the brush. "Did you hear that?" he demanded of Jana. "They're not satisfied with caterwauling that shatters crystal; they've brought in a Chinese drum and bugle corps."

"Calm down, Glen," she soothed. "There weren't any bugles."

"They'll bring 'em. Just watch, they'll be here." His gray eyes switched to Wade, sweeping up and down. "Who's this?"

Jana performed the introductions, explaining that Wade had become involved in the neighborhood problem.

Glen pointed a long finger at a spot behind Jana. "What's that?"

She stepped aside. "That's what you heard. I'm using it to fight fire with fire."

"You mean you made that infernal racket?"

"Uh-huh. But don't knock it until you see what it does. In fact, if you hang around a bit, you'll get a firsthand demonstration."

From the trees above came a prolonged soprano gargle. A chunky woman in a red jumpsuit and sneakers drifted into view. She was in a sitting position, folded in a V, with her legs straddling the rope. Her toes were almost as high as her head and her bottom was definitely the southernmost part.

"She's too low," Glen stated objectively.

"She's perfect," Jana disagreed. "You know," she added, puzzled, "this group hasn't come along very fast. I'd think by now they'd be better than this."

Glen watched the woman's descent. "It's a weekend group. They figure if they make it in four weekends, they're doing well. And it usually takes them..."

Jana listened absently, gauging the woman's speed. Glen was still talking when she thumped the gong a second time. He jumped and turned, almost falling in his haste to express his feelings. He was distracted by the sight of Jana and Wade staring at the woman. His gaze followed theirs.

The woman made a perfect landing. Distracted by the noise, her hands slipped and she dropped gently to the ground. As Glen had noted, she was far too low; she fell only a few inches. That fact, however, did nothing to improve her temper. She jumped to her feet in a fury.

Jana hunkered down by the thicker foliage. The two men followed.

The woman glared, kicked at some bushes, slapped the dust from her bottom, grabbed the dangling rope and stomped back through the weeds.

Jana stood up as soon as she disappeared. She looked at Glen, who had followed suit. "Well?"

The corners of his mouth quirked. "Can I do the next one?" he asked.

Wade nudged the gong with the toe of his shoe. "How long are you planning to hide in the weeds banging on this thing?"

"As long as it takes," she assured him.

"I'll help," Glen offered, grabbing for the stick.

Wade frowned. "It's not going to work."

Jana handed over the stick, biting back a smile at the gratified expression in the older man's eyes. "Sure it will," she told Wade. "It's called behavior modification, remember? They'll get tired of falling down. Pretty soon they won't want to run the risk. Then they'll do something else."

"Listen!" Glen instructed. "It sounds like they're already having an argument down there. I think there's mutiny in the ranks." His shoulders shook. "I'd love to see Benny's face."

Jana looked at him curiously. "I've never met her. What's she like?"

"Benny?" He fiddled with the frame of the gong. When he answered, he sounded surprised. "Nice. Very nice. But when she gets a bee in her bonnet, like this crazy business," he gestured at the trees, "she'll do what she wants, come hell or high water."

He sat down on a tree stump. "It's not that she's deliberately trying to drive us nuts. At least, I don't think so. She just has tunnel vision. She thinks this is the best way to work with those people, and she'll fight tooth and nail for the right to do it." He snorted. "Hell, I can't even accuse her of doing it for the money. She's got more than she knows what to do with. Probably just charges them a token amount.

Which means," he added gloomily, "that there'll be a waiting list a mile long for people to come up here."

Taking out a handkerchief and wiping his head, he added, "Benny's always talking about being on the cutting edge of things. She believes that this is the treatment of the future." He looked appalled as he considered his words. "Do you realize that if she has a high success rate with this crazy scheme, she'll be bringing in people—scientists, I mean—to show them how it works? And she'll never stop."

Wade cut him off briskly. "We'll just have to fix it so it doesn't work, won't we?"

Glen eyed the gong longingly. "Right. And we'll start with the next person that cuts through those branches."

"Wrong," Wade said, retrieving the padded stick from atop the frame where Glen had placed it and stuffing it into his back pocket.

"Wrong?" Jana and Glen said at the same time, in the same disgruntled tone.

He nodded. "For a couple of reasons. First, as soon as they grow accustomed to the sound of that thing, it'll lose its effect. You need to keep them off balance with a variety of things. Second, sitting out here waiting for them to fly by so you can beat on that thing is like chipping words on stone when you have a typewriter on hand."

Jana stirred restlessly. "What do you have in mind?"

"Just updating your idea a bit."

Glen searched the trees with an anxious glance. "I think someone's going to try it. Give me the stick. Quick!"

Wade shook his head. "No way."

"What do you mean?"

"Right now," Wade said evenly, "only two of them have experienced this thing. It'll be better to leave it at that tonight."

"One more won't hurt," Glen said stubbornly. "Come on, Masters, give me the stick."

"Nope."

The two men glared at each other, then turned to Jana.

She hadn't taken her eyes off Wade. "What do you mean, updating? What do you know about behavior modification?"

He sighed in exasperation. "Not a damn thing. But I do know about electronics."

"Electronics?" She repeated the word as if she had never before encountered it. "What does that have to do with anything?"

"You do happen to remember what I do for a living, don't you?" he inquired in far too gentle a tone.

"Sure. You manufacture a lot of scientific gadgets and you specialize in electric eyes." She reeled off the words automatically, much as a child does when reciting the alphabet or multiplication tables.

"You're not making this easy, are you?" he asked grimly. "All right, we'll do it the slow way. What do electric eyes do?"

"Open and close supermarket doors," she said promptly.

"Anything else?"

"Lots of things," she said vaguely. "I suppose."

"Set off burglar alarms," Glen contributed from the tree stump.

"Precisely." The answer, so simply given, so softly spoken, brought Jana's eyes to his.

"And other kinds of alarms?" she asked tentatively.

He nodded, a smile lighting his eyes long before it reached his lips.

"You mean you could rig something up to replace me and this overgrown cymbal?" she asked in growing excitement.

He nodded again, grinning.

Glen looked up, intrigued. "What exactly can you do with it?"

Wade politely tried to cover his surprise at the question. "What kind of work are you in?" he asked the older man.

"Retired. Sales. Never got involved with scientific stuff. I'm beginning to think I missed a good thing."

"What can it do?" Jana repeated impatiently.

"Honey," Wade said lazily, "it can do anything I'm smart enough to make it do. And," he added dryly, "I'm smart."

"Well, what are we waiting for?" she asked. "Let's get to work. You guys help me get this," she patted the gong, "back to the house, then we'll talk."

"Are you sure you don't want me to whack it just once when the next body comes by?" Glen inquired.

Jana's frown, matched by Wade's, was answer enough.

He shrugged sheepishly. "Just asking."

The two men made light work of transporting the gong. They parked it at the gazebo, where they all sat down for a council of war.

"I don't want anyone hurt," Jana said anxiously. "That's why I was willing to sit out there and bang on that thing at just the right moment."

Wade agreed. "No problem. I can line it up so they'll drop from the lowest point."

"Aunt Tillie'd really be upset if anything happened to them," she worried.

"Trust me, honey; I'll take care of it."

Jana was suddenly curious to see Wade on his own turf. She had unintentionally dragged him from one situation where he seemed to be the new kid on the block to another. Even so, he had handled himself well. More than well. Admit it, she told herself, you're impressed.

Now he had the look of a man who was back in his own element, fielding questions with competence, asking his own and assimilating the answers with a slightly abstracted air. Already he was planning. She could almost see the wheels turning as he queried Glen about the physical layout beyond Tillie's house. Yes, she decided, knowing there had never really been any doubt, he was a man she could trust.

Wade asked Glen about the neighbors. "Will they help?"

"Will a starving man eat?" he answered. "What do you need?"

Frowning at the gong, Wade said, "I need something beside that. Something noisy, with impact."

Glen studied the floorboards between his feet. "For tapes?"

Jana decided he was catching on quickly for a nonscientist.

"Yes."

"You need Ferreli," he said with certainty. In reply to Wade's questioning look, he added, "Last neighbor around the bend. Used to be a special effects man in Hollywood. Has a tape library of all his films. Some of the most hair-raising stuff you've ever heard."

"Good." He had one last question for the older man. "Are you a night owl?"

"I will be tonight."

The two men seemed to be communicating through their pores, Jana thought. A lot was being decided with very few words. She wasn't the least bit surprised when they both rose and looked down at her with "goodbye" written all over their faces.

"Wait a minute," she said. "What are you two going to do?"

"I'm going home to pick up a few essentials," Wade said. "Glen is going to let the neighbors know that we'll be prowling around tonight, and he'll meet me in about an hour and introduce me to Mr. Ferreli."

"Well, what am *I* going to do?"

Wade wrapped his arm around her shoulder, urging her down the gazebo stairs and toward the house. "You," he instructed softly, "are going to watch television with Tillie for a while, then go to bed and get a good night's sleep."

"You're going to need help, aren't you?" she protested.

"I will. And I'll get it—from Glen." He looked at her mutinous face and added dryly, "I'm going to need my wits about me tonight, and Glen is a hell of a lot less distracting." He opened the back door and dropped a quick, hard kiss on her lips. "Get that sleep," he ordered. "I want you to enjoy tomorrow."

And sleep she did. But not until she paced the floor a bit and lay in bed wide-eyed, watching the moon work its way across her window. Four months? she wondered. Could she possibly work miracles in four months? Or less? A master plan, she decided, was a pain in the neck. Especially when a man like Wade Masters strolled into one's life and made scrambled eggs of it.

Her sigh was a blend of acceptance and anticipation. It was perfectly obvious that she wasn't able to say goodbye to the man. The only thing she could do, she informed herself sleepily, was to rearrange her life to include him. She turned over on her stomach, flattening the pillow with the side of her head. And why on earth did that decision seem so reasonable tonight when last week it hadn't even been among her options?

Shortly after dawn Wade crossed quietly to his car, looking at the dark windows of the front bedroom where Jana lay sleeping. He turned the key in the ignition and quietly rolled down the street. The night had been long, but satisfying. Everything was set up for tomorrow. What was even more important, he had reached a decision.

Jana Cantrell belonged to him, and to him only. She might not know it yet, but she would. Soon. However, he had been guilty of rushing her, and she was obviously not a woman to be rushed. So, beginning tomorrow, he would back up a step or two and give her some space. Not a hell of a lot, but some.

He pulled up in his driveway, got out of the car and slammed the door a bit harder than was necessary.

Tomorrow was another day—not a day to reach out and grab what he wanted, though—a day to prove once and for all that he was a patient man.

Chapter Ten

Enjoy the day. That's what he had said, Jana fumed to herself early the next afternoon as she sat eating lunch with Tillie. How was she supposed to do that if she didn't know what was happening? Or when. Or how. Men! she thought in disgust. Why on earth she had remained awake all hours of the night speculating about one of them was beyond her.

She had called his house all morning, leaving increasingly acerbic messages on his answering machine. Her hazel eyes brightened with satisfaction as she remembered her final one. Glen Franks had also disappeared, she mused, returning to her list of annoyances. He was neither in his beloved garden nor on the special strip of putting green he had in his backyard. And since she had not yet met his wife, Jana drew the line at pounding on his door and demanding to know his whereabouts.

Jana looked up to meet her aunt's inquiring gaze. "Did you say something, Aunt Tillie?"

There was an inquisitive expression in her bright blue eyes that didn't match her placid tone. "Some more fruit?" She waved at a dish brimming with fresh strawberries, pineapple and melon. As Jana nodded and held out her plate, Tillie asked idly, "Do you have any plans for today?"

Good question. Wade knew. Glen knew. But they weren't telling. "I'm not sure," she answered vaguely. "Wade said he'd drop by later. Why? Is there anything you need help with?"

"As a matter of fact, yes. I was going to ask you to get some extra patio chairs out of the garage and dust them for me."

"How many?"

"Ten or so. Yes, I think ten will be just fine."

"Are you expecting company?" Silly question. Who else would use the chairs? But her aunt never organized parties. She maintained that more than enough people dropped by without invitations.

Tillie considered the question. "I haven't invited anyone," she said carefully. Her bright eyes lingered on Jana's face, as if searching for the answer to an unspoken question.

Jana put down her fork. "But you know they're coming?"

"Walter said something last night about visitors."

Jana found her aunt's steady regard a bit nerve-racking. "Was he, ah, worried about anything?"

Tillie's voice was tranquil. "He said I would be meeting some of my neighbors tonight."

If he knew what was going on, and that was all he had said, Walter was becoming a master of understatement, Jana decided. Of course, he had already informed Tillie that the situation would be resolved. He probably just wasn't involving himself in the details.

Jana touched her lips with the napkin. "I'll take care of the chairs now." She left before any of the questions trembling on her aunt's lips could be voiced.

The afternoon dragged on for several days. Not wanting to miss Wade's call—assuming, of course, that he was going to return one of her sixteen messages—Jana went no farther than the backyard. Tillie joined her, pointing out some weeds that had been missed by the gardener. Jana took her frustration out on those few green tendrils and looked around for more. She nodded as Tillie chatted gently, describing the latest episode in the battle of the thrips. Her aunt must be at least one step ahead of them, she decided, because the roses were magnificent, spilling their perfume into the warm air.

Shortly after three she went to the kitchen to glare at the telephone and get a glass of water. On the third swallow the phone rang. She disposed of the glass and reached for it.

"You wanted to talk to me?" asked an unmistakable voice.

For once the primary feeling generated by that voice was irritation. "Got my message, did you?"

"Which one?" His deep chuckle was maddening, she decided.

"Will you please tell me where you are, what you've been doing and—" she lowered her voice as Tillie came into view "—what on earth is going on around here?"

"At home, sleeping, and that's what I called to tell you."

"*Sleeping?* How can you sleep on a day like this?"

"It's easy when you don't get to bed until six in the morning," he said dryly.

"Six?" She leaned back against the wall. "What on earth were you doing all that time?"

"Getting things set up for today."

"So today is D day? For sure?"

"Absolutely. About five-thirty. That's when they took flight last night, wasn't it?"

"I think so."

"Okay, that's it, then." He paused before adding uncertainly, "You don't mind if some of the neighbors drop by, do you? They want to be..."

"In on the kill?" she asked sweetly.

"It's only the ones whose property borders Benny's. Five couples, ten people."

Jana smiled, anticipating his reaction. "A few hours ago, Aunt Tillie had me pull ten chairs out of the garage."

There was a strangled oath on the other end of the line. Wade finally said, "You know I think the world of Tillie, but even you have to admit that sometimes she's...spooky."

"That's a perfect word for it," Jana agreed cheerfully. "I've often said the same thing."

"Oh." His surprise, and relief, were obvious. "About tonight. What do you think of that area where we were last night? We can see, but we won't be seen."

Jana nodded. "Good idea. Those poor people are going to have enough on their hands without the added humiliation of a visible audience."

"I'll be over at about five," he said, and hung up.

Jana slowly replaced the receiver. Her job, she gathered, was to inform Aunt Tillie of the invasion to take place, and the reason for it.

When she finally brought it up, Tillie surprised her. "I know we're having company, dear. I asked you to bring out extra chairs, remember?"

"But do you know *why* they're coming?"

"Something to do with the trees, I imagine." Her tone implied that as far as she was concerned, the problem was over and done with.

"As a matter of fact, it is," Jana said in surprise.

"That's nice," Tillie said absently, frowning as she scrutinized the underside of a rose leaf. "Walter did say it would be taken care of, remember?"

Jana sighed. "I remember."

Wade arrived promptly at five, and almost on his heels came Glen and his attractive, gray-haired wife. The Simmonses, both tall and tanned, came with several bottles of chilled wine. The Raleys, Greenes and Ferrelis strolled in together, bearing brown sacks with an assortment of chips and dips and more wine. Tillie had dressed for the party in a bilious burgundy jumpsuit. Only Mr. Green, who was an interior decorator, winced.

Introductions were sketchily made and the safari began. The men hauled chairs and tables to the bower behind the gazebo. The women followed with the refreshments and glassware. They barely had time to organize the chairs and pour the wine before the show began.

Mr. Bannister led off. His call had improved, Jana noted. It was now quite an assertive "yah-*hoo*."

"He did that quite well, didn't he?" Tillie whispered proudly. Jana nodded and touched her aunt's hand.

The man had gained a certain panache, Jana thought. He still wore the safari suit, boots and headband, but he had lost that petrified look, and his eyes didn't protrude quite so much. Until he crossed the point where Wade had done his handiwork. When a clap of thunder sounding like the crack of doom came from out of nowhere, he cast a look of pure terror to the sky, and he realized he was slipping. The tips of his boots hit the dirt, the rope flipped out of his hands, and he fell face forward, rolling on a cushiony mat of eucalyptus leaves. Leaves clung to his suit and dust covered his boots when he regained his feet. He gazed upward through the branches to the blue, blue sky. He ran his fingers through wispy, brown hair, absently sifting out a few cracked and crumpled leaves. Shaking his head in confusion, he grabbed the rope and turned back to the starting point.

Jana turned to her companions. Wade was narrow-eyed with concentration, obviously evaluating the performance. Tillie empathized with Mr. Bannister. Glen whacked his knee in enjoyment. The rest were bemused, except for Mr. Ferreli. His dark eyes reflected a quiet satisfaction.

Mrs. Benevides was also in better voice. There was less preliminary throat-clearing and very little apology in her call. A ripple of leaves announced the arrival of her bronzed, angular frame. Her coordination was better, Jana decided—at least for a while. When she heard the tumult of trampling feet and the trumpeting of an elephant, she panicked. Her heels hit the ground, gouging a double furrow in the dry soil. Pushing her glasses up her nose, she ran for the largest tree she could find and hid behind it. She reappeared only after the stampede passed and the last emotional elephant vented its vocal spleen.

Peeking around the tree, Mrs. Benevides looked in all directions before tiptoeing out to hook her arm around the rope and take off.

Jana took another visual temperature reading. Wade was relaxed and trying not to grin. Glen's shoulders were shaking. Tillie was still empathizing. Mr. Ferreli was clearly satisfied with his contribution, and the rest were having a hard time subduing snickers and giggles.

The soprano gargler came next. She had washed her red jumpsuit and was still folded up in a V.

"That's Mrs. Ryan," Tillie whispered. "Nice lady, but such a temper."

The nice lady was looking up at the sky and that might have been her downfall, mused Jana. When she heard a loud, ominous crack and the sound of splitting wood, the sight of leaves drifting downward made it seem all too real. With a loud gasp she let go of the rope and once again landed bottom first in the dirt. Clearly expecting the thick branch to collapse, she dropped flat and rolled to the side, coming to rest in a prickly bush.

She sat up and eyed the dangling rope, then the branch far above. Struggling to her feet, the chunky woman kicked wrathfully at the spiny shrub and reached back to loosen the most painful stickers. Once again her eyes followed the rope up to the stout branch.

Mrs. Ryan didn't lack spunk. Jana had to give her that. She darted to the center of the clearing, snagged the rope and didn't stop until she was at the far side, well out from beneath the branch. She gave the rope a tentative tug. When the branch didn't give, she pulled harder. And harder. Her face grew red and she uttered infuriated little grunts each time she tugged. Finally realizing that the branch wasn't going to budge, she gave the rope a furious swing and hauled it away. She began yelling for Benny before she was even out of sight.

Mr. Simmons reached for a bottle of wine and refilled his glass. "If I had more than one drink, I'd never have believed I saw what I just saw."

Glen groped for his handkerchief to wipe his eyes, his brow and his perspiring head.

"I never realized my tapes had such potential," Mr. Ferreli said. "God, what a slapstick comedy that would make." He dropped into a thoughtful coma.

"Funny as all this is, do you think it'll do any good?" Edith Franks asked.

Wade lifted a warning hand. "I think the second act is about to begin." He flicked a button on a slim black stick and looked up to meet Jana's curious gaze. "I don't want anything accidentally tripped off," he explained, putting it in his shirt pocket.

Voices rose in the distance like storm clouds, gathering volume and density as they approached. Jana heard Mr. Bannister's tenor voice for the first time.

"I know it sounds crazy, but I heard thunder."

"Elephants!" Obviously Mrs. Benevides.

Freckles broke through the bushes. "It was right here. Last night. Sounded like a bunch of cymbals."

"I heard it, too," Mrs. Ryan said. "Awful thing. And just a minute ago the branch broke."

"You can see there's nothing here," a small woman said in a carrying voice.

Jana turned to her aunt. "Is that Benny?"

Tillie nodded.

Jana took another look. She had expected an imposing woman, somewhat like a schooner in full sail. But Benny was small, petite, even tiny. But she had the voice of a drill sergeant. She was telling her crew that there was nothing wrong with the tree or anything else.

Four people shuffled through brush and knocked at branches. Jana reached for Wade's hand.

"They won't find anything," he assured her.

Benny leaned against a tree. "Satisfied?" she finally asked.

Four faces scowled at her.

"Okay," she boomed, "let's go back and do it again."

Four pairs of feet rooted themselves to the ground.

"Come on, tigers, let's go do it! You'll make it this time."

Four pairs of ears were deaf to the pep talk.

"One more time. You can do it."

Four sets of stiff shoulders advanced on her.

"If you think for one minute—"

"I wouldn't touch that rope—"

"You weren't here last—"

"Twice now, I've heard—"

Benny took a deep breath but was drowned out by the indignant voices.

"—that I'll get back on that damned thing—"

"—if my hope of salvation—"

"—listening to that god-awful—"

"—these sinister noises and that's—"

"If you fall off a horse, you should always get right back on and ride it," Benny loudly informed them. There was a moment's silence, then the clamor resumed.

"—you're nuts!"

"—depended on it!"

"—noise."

"—two times too many!"

"But there's nothing here," Benny said. "You've looked; you've seen."

Mr. Bannister staunchly defended himself. I don't care if anyone believes me. I heard a clap of thunder that's still ringing in my ears.

"I know you all think I'm crazy," Mrs. Benevides said, "but I heard elephants. The trample of heavy feet and the trumpeting call. I'll hear it till my dying day."

Freckles spoke up. "This place is spooky. I'll never forget what happened here last night."

"Crashing noises and trees breaking," exclaimed Mrs. Ryan. "No more of that stuff for me."

Benny broke through the agitated comments. "Are you going back to give it one more try?" she demanded.

"Not on your life!"

"You think I'm nuts?"

"No way, lady."

"Hardly!"

She glared at the four rebels. They glared back.

She scowled. They scowled.

Suddenly a bubbling sound broke from her throat. Laughter lifted, soared and filled the air. The mutineers gawked as she gradually subdued her mirth. They regarded her big grin with suspicion.

"Congratulations, my friends." Her voice was warm and friendly. "You just passed your assertiveness training class. You don't need ropes; you don't need trees. You did just fine without them, just fine."

"You're not mad?" Freckles ventured.

"Not at all. In fact, I'm damn proud of you. Few people in the outside world will push you as hard as I did. If you can handle me, you can cope with anyone. Come on, this calls for a celebration."

For the first time no one remembered the rope. It was left behind as the five turned and walked away.

Tillie broke the silence. "Just like a good movie," she said with satisfaction. "I do so love a happy ending." She held out her glass, and Mark Simmons filled it to the brim.

Glen rose and waved for silence. "Ladies and gentlemen, I would like to propose a toast to the hero of the hour, Wade Masters."

Glasses were raised, tilted and emptied.

Wade lifted his glass. "To Vince Ferreli and his film collection."

"Hear, hear." More glasses clinked.

Vince stood up. "To our charming hostess."

Seven toasts later, there was little wine and less sobriety to be found. Glen Franks had the floor. "It's what you call a win-win situation. The goofballs won,

Benny won and we won." He looked down at Edith with a puzzled frown. "Or is that called a win-win-win situation?"

She shrugged. "Got me."

Wade cleared his throat. "I hate to ruin my image as hero of the hour, but something has occurred to me."

A number of owlish stares wavered and finally settled on him.

"What we've won is a temporary victory. This bunch has been taken care of, but what about the ones still to come? Do we pull this stunt every time Benny collects another group of corporate underachievers?"

Glen nodded proudly, as if he had sponsored a particularly intelligent child in a spelling bee. He polled the others with his eyes. "He has a real way with words, hasn't he?"

"Did you *hear* his words, Glen?" Vince asked dryly.

"Oh, my God." The simple, heartfelt phrase, slowly spoken, seemed to represent the group's dawning awareness. The festive spirit deflated like a party balloon, sinking to unmitigated gloom. Only Tillie seemed unaffected.

The morose silence that followed was finally broken by footsteps crunching in the brush. Acacia fronds were grappled with and pushed aside. Benny stepped into the clearing with a casual, "Hi guys, I thought you'd be around here somewhere."

Her childlike body and her dark hair hanging in a single braid down her back didn't warrant the fascinated stares she was receiving. Eyeing the table littered with glasses and chips, she inquired mildly,

"Party time?" She pointed a finger at the wine bottles. "Any of that left?"

The men struggled to their feet in belated courtesy, and Mark Simmons drained the last bottle into a clean glass.

Benny waved the men back to their seats, accepted a glass and settled on the tree stump that had been occupied by Glen the night before. Tasting the wine, she nodded approval. "Good. What did you do?" she inquired genially. "Call in some electronic whiz?"

Thirteen blank stares turned to her. Only in Tillie's case was the stare genuine.

"Not that I blame you," she continued after rolling a bit of wine on her tongue and swallowing appreciatively. "I probably would have done the same thing."

The continued silence did not appear to unsettle her. It occurred to Jana that Benny wasn't merely coping; surprise had given her a momentary advantage, and she was loving every minute of it.

"But it wasn't really necessary, you know." Benny smiled at the carefully blank faces. "This group was my last one." She waited for the involuntary stir of interest, then added airily, "For a while."

She studied the yellow spray of a nearby acacia. No one else broke the silence.

"My intention," Benny informed them, "is always to be on the cutting edge. Others are already imitating this." She waved to the trees, her gaze lingering on the dangling rope. "It's already passé. But I've been researching..." Her voice dwindled away.

Eyes brightened and the bland expression changed to avid interest.

"I won't bore you with my studies." To her eternal credit, she suppressed a grin at the mutual expressions of dismay. "But I assure you, it will bear interesting results."

She jumped to her feet and returned the wineglass. "I'm closing up the house for a couple of months, but I'll have someone come out to dismantle the platforms and remove the ropes. Enjoy your summer. I'll see you all when I come back. I think you'll appreciate my new project."

Tillie was mildly interested, Wade appreciative. Jana beamed a silent "bravo" to the small woman for an Oscar-winning performance. The rest were frankly apprehensive. Benny directed a brilliant smile at them and disappeared. Quivering greenery fell into place behind her.

"What do you suppose she's up to now?" Glen broke the heavy silence with his uneasy inquiry.

"I don't give a damn, as long as it's quiet," Vince assured him. "She can practice witchcraft for all I care."

Mark rose from the patio chair and placed his glass on the table. He looked up, his gaze touching the faces of his neighbors. "You know," he admitted with a curious smile, "ever since she installed that damn stuff in the trees, I've been dying to try it."

Vince grinned and tilted his chair back, his eyes alert.

Glen stood up and peered through the acacias. He looked at the dangling rope, his eyes filled with speculation.

Wade's eyes glinted with amusement.

Ralph Raley said slowly, "Our house would be the best place. It's hidden by a copse of oaks. She'd never see us."

Emily Greene jumped up. "If we're all going to have a turn before it gets dark, we've got to hurry!"

Two hours later a bedraggled crew returned to restore Tillie's furniture to the patio. Vince and Ralph had brought more wine, and within minutes they all moved inside. Glen almost brought the evening to an early end when he asked Tillie if he could whack the Chinese gong. He and Mr. Greene spent the evening bidding briskly for the privilege of owning it. Tillie refused all offers.

It was still early when the neighbors poured out the front door to make their way home. Wade stayed to help tidy up.

He moved around the room, shifting the bulky furniture back in place. He was unusually quiet. Jana had noted the fact earlier—as soon as he had arrived, in fact—but had decided that he was concentrating on his electronic wizardry. She'd had no way to confirm it because he spent the evening moving around, talking to the others. Come to think of it, whenever she had looked around for him, he had been on the other side of the room.

Wade was aware of the silence. He could feel Jana's questioning, her speculation, through every pore in his body. If he was going to leave, to give her the space he'd decided she needed, he'd damn well better do it now. Because if he touched her, even looked too closely at the tousled cloud of her hair or her soft lips, he wouldn't be leaving alone.

Being gallant, he decided grimly, had its drawbacks. He wondered how the knights of old had managed without exploding. He didn't want to go. As a matter of fact, he hated the thought of leaving her tonight. What he wanted more than anything was to scoop her up, deposit her in his car, take her home and spend the night making love to her. He wanted her silken body flowing against his, and the tender touch of her hands, teasing, tantalizing.

At the thought of her bare body next to his, a spasm of desire shafted through him. He bit back a curse. It had been years since his body had ached so for a woman. And he was turning his back on the possibility of assuagement. He, damn fool that he was, was planning to walk out that door without even a kiss good-night.

Jana examined Wade's suddenly grim expression. Her eyes widened as he looked at her and muffled a phony yawn.

He grinned halfheartedly. "Sorry. I'm beat."

Beat? As in tired? How much sleep did the man need? If he'd gone to bed at six and slept until three, by her reckoning he'd had nine hours.

She eyed him skeptically as he yawned again. It still looked as phony as false fingernails. He was up to something, and she wished to hell she knew what it was.

"Well," he said with a final jaw-popping yawn, "I think I'll have an early night." He pulled the door open with unmistakable eagerness. "Will I, er, see you at work Monday?"

Jana blinked. Monday? What about tomorrow? Or didn't he remember that there was a day between Saturday and Monday? As far as that went, what about the rest of tonight? Ten-thirty, at least in her opinion, was not the crack of dawn.

"Sure, I'll be there," she said in surprise.

"Good. See you then." He slammed the door.

Jana stared blankly at the door. Would she ever understand this man? She had just decided to meet him halfway, and here he was running out the door.

Did that mean, then, that she should go all the way?

Chapter Eleven

Do you love him?'' Her aunt's voice broke into her reflections.

Jana turned to find Tillie seated comfortably in her favorite high-backed chair. *"Him?"* Dislike frosted the word.

"Ummm." Tillie tilted her head and watched her niece with birdlike curiosity.

"He's a blockhead."

Tillie smiled. "Do you love the blockhead?"

"He's arrogant."

"Probably. Do you love him?"

Jana stretched out on the couch and scowled at her feet. "Do you have any idea how he's disrupted my life in the few weeks that I've known him?"

"No. Do you want to tell me?"

"It would take forever."

"Do you love him?"

Jana closed her eyes and silently begged for mercy. She had forgotten her aunt's broken record routine. Tillie rarely interfered, believing that people usually worked things out for themselves, but when she did, she was merciless. She had the water-dripping-on-stone routine down pat. She would repeat the question until Jana either answered or ran screaming from the room like a lunatic.

"The man is a pain in the neck, and you, dear aunt, are driving me nuts."

Tillie's eyes were bright with affection as she said, "Just one more question, then I'll leave you alone."

"What?" Jana asked with foreboding.

"Do you love him?"

Jana sat up so quickly that she almost fell off the sofa. Glaring at her aunt, she said, "Of course I love him."

"What are you going to do about it?"

"What can I do about it? Didn't you see him when he left tonight? He couldn't get out of here fast enough. And he said he'd see me at work on Monday. That doesn't exactly sound as if he's panting to be with me."

"I think it's sweet."

A reluctant smile curved Jana's lips. "You think everything is sweet."

"He's obviously smitten."

"Smitten my...foot. I've never seen anyone less smitten in my life. A smitten man," she informed her aunt, belaboring the point, "does not run out the door as if the hounds of hell were nipping at his heels."

"But he does watch his love like a hawk, protect her even if she doesn't need protecting, and—"

"You said *love*, Aunt Tillie. That's one of the problems. If he's doing anything, he's lusting, not loving."

"If that's the truth, and it probably is—heaven only knows it was that way with Walter—"

"Uncle Walter *lusted?*" Jana asked, round-eyed.

"He certainly did," Tillie said with a reminiscent smile. "Don't all men? Now where was I?" She frowned. "I was making a point when you interrupted me. Oh, yes. He may have started out lusting, but that's not the way he feels now."

"I wish I could believe that," Jana mumbled.

"You can," Tillie assured her in a serene voice. She gave Jana time to think about that before asking, "What would you do if you believed he loved you?"

"For starters, I wouldn't let him get away with leaving me the way he did tonight."

"Why do you suppose he did it?"

"I don't know," Jana said slowly. "He's been after me from the day we met, telling me I was going to end up in his bed." She shot a glance at her aunt and censored her own words. "Etcetera and so on."

"Etcetera is such a fascinating word," Tillie said placidly. "Do go on."

"And I've been running as fast as I could go. I came to my senses last night and realized that I didn't want to run *from* him. I wanted to run *to* him. And tonight," she said flatly, "he took to his heels."

"Do you think it's possible that he did the same thing?" Tillie asked. "Only in reverse?"

"I beg your pardon?" Jana said blankly. "Would you run that one by me again?"

Tillie spelled it out. "Could he have decided that he was coming on too strong, as they say?" She stopped. "*Is* that what they say?" Jana gave an amused nod and she continued. "And that he should slow down and give you a little room?"

"Space," Jana murmured. The two women sat in companionable silence. "That idiot," Jana observed finally with a slow smile.

"Men do need a helping hand at times," Tillie agreed.

"I can't believe he'd do something like that."

"Believe it," Tillie said.

"It's not at all like him. If I've learned anything at all about him, it's that he's an aggressive man. He goes after what he wants."

Tillie considered the facts calmly. "Would you say he's an intelligent man?"

A smile still curved Jana's lips. "Most of the time."

"A good businessman?"

"Absolutely."

"If he couldn't close a business deal one way, would he find another?"

"You'd better believe it."

"Ah."

Jana slowly got to her feet. "Ah, indeed."

Tillie picked up the paper and looked at the television log. "There's a science fiction film just starting. I think I'll watch it. What are you going to do?"

Jana moved to the door. "I think I'll give a certain man a helping hand." She stopped and looked back. "I might not be back tonight, Aunt Tillie."

Tillie flipped the channels until she saw a lizardlike monster stomping buildings in Tokyo. "How old are you now, dear?"

Jana smiled. "Twenty-six."

"Old enough," Tillie murmured, and moved back to her chair, not wanting to miss a single toppling building.

Jana tore into her bedroom and threw open the closet door. "Clothes," she muttered. "What on earth will I wear?" This could be the most momentous evening of her life and what was in the closet? Nothing! Not one slinky number, not even a charming, girl-next-door dress.

"Calm down, Jana," she advised herself. "Let's just see what's here." Nothing. Shorts, blouses, knit shirts, a poncho, a couple of skirts. Bor-ing.

All right, try it again. Slowly this time. Remember that necessity is the mother of invention and all that other stuff. Think, for heaven's sake! Unless you want to drive home? No, that'll take another hour at least. Shifting coat hangers, she scrutinized each item of clothing. Her hand stopped on one and she lifted it out, her eyes full of speculation.

The poncho?

Thirty minutes later, running on adrenaline, she was pressing her finger on Wade's doorbell. There were lights on, so she knew he was still up. She removed her finger, and the full realization of what she was doing hit her. This was the big seduction scene, right? Right. She was going to go in there and knock his socks off, right? Right. She... What on earth *was* she going to do in there? she wondered wretchedly. She knew absolutely zip about seducing a man. Just about the time she was deciding that she belonged anywhere except where she was, Wade answered the door.

She hadn't remembered that he almost filled the doorway.

"Jana! What are you doing here?"

Not a very loverlike greeting, she noted absently. She was still trying to figure out what she was going to do when he let her in. *If* he let her in. She frankly doubted that she had the courage to follow through with her original plan.

Wade was clearly waiting for an answer. He hadn't budged an inch. "I was just passing by," she said mendaciously, "and thought I'd drop in to say hello."

Wade moved back reluctantly, watching her through narrowed eyes. He wasn't in the best of moods. It had been hard enough to get himself out of Tillie's house alone. And he had just been brooding over a painfully learned lesson. Being noble did not relieve aching, wanting and needing. Neither did the sight of her prancing through his front door wearing—what the hell *was* she wearing?

"What are you wearing?" he demanded.

"The poncho you gave me." She walked into the large, welcoming room and turned slowly, imitating a model's swaying glide. "Like it?"

Her bare feet were in high-heeled thongs. His eyes traced over trim ankles, smooth calves, pretty knees and a couple of inches of thigh. From that point up to her neck was poncho. "Very nice," he grunted, and took a swallow of the drink in his hand.

She reached for the glass, tugged, and when he released it, took a sip. "Iced tea?" she inquired blankly, returning it. "According to all the books I read, you should be drinking brandy."

"You probably read abominable stuff. Besides, I don't like brandy," he said reasonably.

Now what? she wondered. No brandy... therefore not half-intoxicated and easily led astray. Instead he was full of iced tea, clearheaded and probably very stubborn and puritanical. She wondered if Delilah had ever had days like this.

Wade put the glass on the table and rested his hands on his hips. A grin curved his lips. He couldn't help it. She looked so damned cute examining the books on the shelves with that black fringed poncho flirting around her thighs.

"Jana," he said gently, "what are you doing here?"

"Well, actually, I," she cleared her throat, "I'm here to seduce you."

"The hell you are," he said blankly.

Now what does one say to a statement like that? she wondered in mounting irritation. Nothing, absolutely nothing, was going the way she had planned.

"What do you know about seduction?" he asked, his annoyance matching hers.

"Not much," she admitted readily. "I was hoping you'd sort of help me along."

"Well, I won't." He moved behind a chair as she approached him. "In fact, I think you ought to go home."

"I told Aunt Tillie I wouldn't be back tonight," she said absently, wondering how to flush him out from behind the chair.

"You *what?*" he asked in an outraged tone.

Enough was enough, Jana decided. He'd stand there all night and talk if she let him. She dipped her hands beneath the poncho and felt for her waist.

Wade watched in fascination as the poncho bulged with the movement of her arms. She brought out a navy-blue piece of material and dropped it on the floor.

"What's that?" he asked hoarsely.

"A wraparound skirt," she said, pulling her hands back under the poncho. This time it took a bit longer. She was dealing with buttons and tie strings. She finally brought out a white, gauzy piece of fabric. It also drifted to the floor.

"Blouse," she explained gently.

Wade was breathing heavily, and no longer behind the chair, she noted with satisfaction.

Her hands disappeared, made one quick motion and emerged with a strapless wisp of material. She made no explanation as it slowly joined the clothes on the floor.

Her eyes locked with his as she reached for one of the large, shiny buttons at the neck of the poncho. She released the first, then the second. One creamy shoulder was now showing. His gaze dropped down.

"For God's sake, Jana," he groaned. "What do you have on under that?"

"Not very much," she admitted honestly. She moved to him, standing so close that she could feel the heat from his body. Her eyes, wide and honest, met his as she said, "I want you, Wade, in every way that a woman can want a man. I *need* you."

He drew her against him. Summoning the last bit of strength he had in reserve, his hands remained outside the poncho, but his lips explored the soft, fragrant skin exposed by the open buttons. "You don't know how hard it was for me to leave you tonight," he told her in a rough voice. "But I had decided that I'd rushed you. I needed to give you more space."

"I don't want space," she murmured. "I want you." Her arms wrapped around his neck, providing him with a fascinating view as the open neck of the poncho dipped.

Wade bent his head, covered her honeyed lips with his own. Women, he thought hazily as he released the third button, usually dreamed of large weddings. With luck, and if he locked his tempting little love up in a suit of armor, he might just last six more hours. He'd never last six months, or even weeks. He wondered how she felt about—— He almost dropped Jana when the telephone rang.

He didn't have a doubt in the world whose voice he would hear when he picked up the receiver. Jana was a delectable sight. Her face was dazed and soft with love. Her hair was gloriously disheveled. And what was possibly her last item of clothing was beginning to ease down over the curve of one breast.

If Tillie could see down telephone wires, could she also summon up a picture of fringed, black ponchos? "For God's sake," he hissed to his bemused love, "button that thing up!"

Turning his back on her, Wade reached for the shrilling telephone. "Hello," he snarled.

"Wade, dear, I know this isn't the best time to call, but Walter wanted me to reassure you. Las Vegas would be just fine. There could always be a nice reception later. Oh, and he said to look for the Wee Little Chapel in the Kirk. That's where we went. Or was it the dell? Or it might have been the Wee Little—"

"I'll find it," he promised her gently, then replaced the receiver. He turned back to Jana. "Where were we?" he asked.

She smiled brilliantly from the security of a buttoned poncho. "We were seducing each other."

He advanced on her, and she realized that that look was back in his eyes—the proprietary one that had always before sent her scurrying. Even now... She suddenly realized that the seduction had been taken out of her hands.

"Two hours," Wade murmured against her lips. "If we fly. We can be married in Las Vegas." He had just discovered that the poncho wasn't the only thing she had on. There was a silky band about an inch wide on her hips that...

"Are we getting married?" she asked dreamily. "I had my heart set on being a Wicked Woman."

"You still can," he promised, his thumb following the patch of silk. "In two hours."

Epilogue

Jana curled up next to Wade's naked body in the king-size bed. Her head was tucked in the hollow of his shoulder. Being a Wicked Woman, she thought for the thousandth time, was not so difficult. She had learned that much in the last nine months. No, actually, the realization had come much sooner. That first night, after they left the Wee Little Kirk in the Wildwood, or was it the Wee Little Dell in the Kirk? Whatever. She had found that twenty-six years of waiting had honed her natural instincts.

Once they had returned home, two sets of parents and assorted brothers and sisters with their families had converged for the promised reception. The only time Wade had put his foot down was to state adamantly that the Romero brothers were not to sing at the affair.

Her fingers drifted over the tawny mat of hair on Wade's chest as she thought of her aunt's birthday party the night before. Dane had hovered over Kara, his silvery green eyes protective and soft. No one had been surprised when they announced that there would be a little Logan at Aunt Tillie's next birthday party.

Jana traced the soft, prickly hair down to Wade's stomach. Amazing how it narrowed down, right there, then fanned out again. Dane and Kara had also announced that the Romero brothers had taken Tijuana by storm. Much to the surprise of the brothers, the *Cantores Sin Iqualidad* were being hailed as the greatest comedy act to hit town in years.

Why had she worried about work? she wondered, moving her hand to the inside of his thigh. There had been no insurmountable problems. Hiring someone to clean the house and cook an evening meal had resolved almost everything. Everything was just perfect, she decided—or it would be if Wade would just wake up.

Wade shifted slightly, bringing his arm down and cupping Jana's pert breast with his hand. He luxuriated in the unbelievably tender touch of a woman's caressing fingers. *His* woman's touch, he amended firmly. He smiled as the silken spray of her hair tickled his chest.

Brown eyes opened to meet a speculative hazel gaze.

Jana curved her lips in a soft, deeply feminine smile. "You're awake."

"Um-hmm." His hand followed a trail of fascinating hollows and curves.

She moved slightly, rubbing her leg against his. "I'm glad."

He smiled. "Me too."

"I love you," she whispered.

His eyes darkened. "I know."

"That's not an appropriate answer," she informed him in her best professional voice. "You're supposed to tell me that you reciprocate."

He turned, easing over her. "You know I do. Every hour of every day. Every minute of every hour."

Her eyes darkened. "I know," she whispered in deep contentment. "I know."

You won't want to miss a single one of the heart-felt stories presented by Silhouette Special Edition; and when you take advantage of this special offer, you won't have to.

You'll also receive a FREE subscription to the Silhouette Books Newsletter as long as you remain a member. Each lively issue is filled with news on upcoming titles, interviews with your favorite authors, even their favorite recipes.

To become a home subscriber and receive your first 4 books FREE, fill out and mail the coupon today!

Silhouette Special Edition®

Silhouette Books, 120 Brighton Rd., P.O. Box 5084, Clifton, NJ 07015-5084

AMERICAN TRIBUTE

Where a man's dreams count for more than his parentage...

Look for these upcoming titles under the Special Edition American Tribute banner.

LOVE'S HAUNTING REFRAIN
Ada Steward #289—February 1986
For thirty years a deep dark secret kept them apart—King Stockton made his millions while his wife, Amelia, held everything together. Now could they tell their secret, could they admit their love?

THIS LONG WINTER PAST
Jeanne Stephens #295—March 1986
Detective Cody Wakefield checked out Assistant District Attorney Liann McDowell, but only in his leisure time. For it was the danger of Cody's job that caused Liann to shy away.

AM-TRIB-1

Silhouette *Special Edition*

★ ★ AMERICAN ★ TRIBUTE ★ ★ ★

AMERICAN TRIBUTE

RIGHT BEHIND THE RAIN
Elaine Camp #301—April 1986
The difficulty of coping with her brother's
death brought reporter Raleigh Torrence
to the office of Evan Younger, a police
psychologist. He helped her to deal with
her feelings and emotions, including love.

CHEROKEE FIRE
Gena Dalton #307—May 1986
It was Sabrina Dante's silver spoon that
Cherokee cowboy Jarod Redfeather couldn't
trust. The two lovers came from opposite
worlds, but Jarod's Indian heritage taught
them to overcome their differences.

NOBODY'S FOOL
Renee Roszel #313—June 1986
Everyone bet that Martin Dante and Cara
Torrence would get together. But Martin
wasn't putting any money down, and Cara
was out to prove that she was nobody's fool.

MISTY MORNINGS, MAGIC NIGHTS
Ada Steward #319—July 1986
The last thing Carole Stockton wanted was to
fall in love with another politician, especially
Donnelly Wakefield. But under a blanket of
secrecy, far from the campaign spotlights,
their love became a powerful force.

Silhouette Romance

COMING NEXT MONTH

TO CATCH A THIEF—Brittany Young
Michal went to Paris with one intention—to steal back her grandmother's chalices that were auctioned off to Frenchman Phillippe Dumas. She hired a "professional" thief—who ended up stealing her heart.

WILD HORIZONS—Frances Lloyd
Returning to Australia to claim ownership of his family's outback ranch, Chad planned to claim Marla, as well. But what about the scandal that had forced him to leave ten years ago?

YESTERDAY'S HERO—Debbie Macomber
Nothing would keep Leah or Cain from missing an expedition to study the ancient whales of the Diamantina Islands. But why would a business trip have to include marriage?

ROSES NEVER FADE—Raye Morgan
In the middle of a stormy northern California night, a handsome stranger walked into the foyer of Bailey Trent's supposedly haunted house. He was certainly no ghost, but who was he?

A MAN OF CHARACTER—Barbara Bartholomew
While running the family farm, Cath was quickly falling for Doug. He was no typical farmhand...but he was very mysterious. What had happened in his past that he was refusing to reveal?

ANGEL AND THE SAINT—Emilie Richards
Angelle and Kyle had nothing in common, except that each were trying to adopt an orphaned child. But an earthly act of love might turn into a marriage made in heaven.

AVAILABLE THIS MONTH:

THE PERFECT TOUCH
Rita Rainville

A SILENT SONG
Lacey Springer

ONCE UPON A TIME
Lucy Gordon

REASON ENOUGH
Arlene James

CROSSWINDS
Curtiss Ann Matlock

BEWITCHED BY LOVE
Brenda Trent